Dear Reader,

It's been years since I visited Italy, but three things have stayed with me despite the passage of time: the friendliness of the people, the beauty of the Italian countryside, and the food.

Oh, the food. I've often said if I were allowed to eat only one kind of cuisine for the rest of my life I would choose Italian.

So when I was asked to be part of *The Brides of Bella Rosa* continuity, I was excited that it not only explored the themes of forgiveness and family, but that it did it so against the backdrop of Rosa and Sorella, the fictional restaurants owned by Luca Casali and his sister Lisa Firenzi.

I invite you to pour yourself a glass of wine and join Atlanta and Angelo as they travel to Italy and toward love.

Happy reading!

Jackie Braun

THE BRIDES *of* BELLA ROSA

Romance, rivalry and a family reunited.

For years Lisa Firenzi and Luca Casali's
sibling rivalry has disturbed the quiet, sleepy Italian
town of Monta Correnti, and their two feuding
restaurants have divided the market square.

Now, as the keys to the restaurants are
handed down to Lisa's and Luca's children,
will history repeat itself? Can the next generation
undo its parents' mistakes, reunite the families
and ultimately join the two restaurants?

Or are there more secrets to be revealed…?

*The doors to the restaurants are open,
so take your seats and look out for secrets,
scandals and surprises on the menu!*

The saga concludes next month in
Firefighter's Doorstep Baby
by Barbara McMahon

JACKIE BRAUN

America's Star-Crossed Sweethearts

THE BRIDES
of
BELLA ROSA

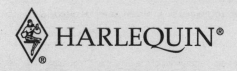

TORONTO • NEW YORK • LONDON
AMSTERDAM • PARIS • SYDNEY • HAMBURG
STOCKHOLM • ATHENS • TOKYO • MILAN • MADRID
PRAGUE • WARSAW • BUDAPEST • AUCKLAND

Recycling programs
for this product may
not exist in your area.

ISBN-13: 978-0-373-17686-1

AMERICA'S STAR-CROSSED SWEETHEARTS

First North American Publication 2010

Copyright © 2010 by Harlequin Books S.A.

Special thanks and acknowledgment are given to Jackie Braun for her contribution to the Brides of Bella Rosa series.

This edition published by arrangement with Harlequin Books S.A.

For questions and comments about the quality of this book please contact us at Customer_eCare@Harlequin.ca.

® and TM are trademarks of the publisher. Trademarks indicated with ® are registered in the United States Patent and Trademark Office, the Canadian Trade Marks Office and in other countries.

www.eHarlequin.com

Printed in U.S.A.

Jackie Braun is a three-time RITA® Award finalist, a four-time National Readers' Choice Award finalist and a past winner of the Rising Star Award. She worked for nearly two decades as an award-winning journalist before leaving her full-time job to write fiction. She lives in mid-Michigan with her husband and their two sons. She loves to hear from readers and can be reached through her Web site at www.jackiebraun.com.

For Brady Williamson and his new sister, Alexandria

PROLOGUE

ANGELO CASALI stood at the home plate with his feet planted shoulder's width apart in the dust. The bat hovered in the air just beyond his right ear. It was the bottom of the ninth inning with two outs, and the Rogues were trailing by two. Anxious runners filled the bases waiting for New York's Angel to work a miracle. They and the fans knew the team's pennant hopes rested squarely on his shoulders.

The opposing team's pitcher glared at Angelo from beneath the bill of his cap. Kyle Morris had one of the best arms in the league. Only a handful of batters could touch his fastball. Angelo was one of them, which was why Morris had yet to bring the heat against him this game. In fact, the pitcher had walked Angelo his last two times at bat. Morris couldn't afford to do that now, and they both knew it.

The pitcher hiked up his leg and levered back his arm before bringing it around. The ball blasted free of his hand like a bullet clearing the barrel of a gun. Even so, Angelo was ready, his eyes tracking its trajectory. He timed his swing perfectly and put everything he had into it, shifting his weight to his right leg as he brought the bat around.

Crack!

The sound of red-stitched white leather meeting wood rent the air like gunfire. It was followed by a sickening *pop!* that only Angelo heard…and felt. Pain, wicked and white-hot, exploded from his shoulder. The crowd's deafening roar drowned out his cry.

It's worth it, he told himself. It's worth it.

Even as he dropped the bat and started toward first base, he knew there was no need to hurry. The ball was riding high in the clouds and showed no signs of dropping.

"And it's out of here!" the announcer shouted.

The fans were on their feet, clapping and high-fiving.

"Angel! Angel! Angel!"

Their jubilant chanting buoyed him. Along with the adrenaline streaking through his system, it allowed him to ignore the worst of the pain. He rounded the bases at a leisurely trot with his good arm raised in triumph. By the time he arrived at home plate, his teammates were out of the dugout, standing there en masse to greet him with whoops and careless back slaps that nearly sent Angelo to his knees. He kept his grin in place, enjoying the moment. How could he not? The Rogues had just sealed a berth in the playoffs. He was the city's hero.

Barely twenty-four hours, Angelo adjusted the ice pack on his shoulder and drank a beer in the solitude of his Upper East Side apartment. If he closed his eyes, he could still hear the crowd chanting his name as the video replayed on the big screen over the scoreboard. He'd watched it from the bench in the dugout, a spot he'd most likely keep warm for what little remained of the season. Most disturbing of all, though, was the thought that this time he might have to hang up his cleats for good.

He sipped the pricey imported brew he'd acquired a taste for his first year in the majors. What would he do then? The question nagged at him more than the pain from his shoulder.

His cell phone trilled as he debated having another drink in lieu of the medication the team doctor had prescribed. It was probably another journalist. Reporters were eager for an interview or even just a quote from the Angel. He snatched it off the coffee table, intending to turn it off. A glance at the readout stopped him. It was his brother, Alessandro.

He grinned as he flipped it open. "Alex. Hey."

"How are you?"

"Never better," Angelo lied.

"Except for your shoulder, you mean."

"Yeah." He shrugged the body part in question and immediately winced. "Except for that. What are you up to?"

"Drinking a beer. Been a long day."

"I'm doing the same. I know what you mean."

Angelo tossed the ice pack aside and started for the kitchen to retrieve another bottle. He wished his twin were there to share a cold one with him in person. It still amazed Angelo that Alex owned a ranch in San Antonio, Texas, and was as at home roping steer as Angelo was snapping up grounders in a major league ballpark. God knew their chaotic childhood hadn't lent itself to either profession. For that matter, it was amazing either of them had amounted to much of anything.

"So, is your shoulder as bad as the sportscasters are saying?" Alex wanted to know.

Angelo made a dismissive sound. "You know how those vultures are. They're milking the story to boost their sagging ratings."

His brother wasn't fooled. "You won't be back in uniform this season."

"No."

"And next year?"

"Sure. After surgery and some rehab I'll be as good as new." Angelo's shoulder throbbed, seemingly in contradiction. He silenced it with a gulp of beer and settled back into the leather recliner. "I'm too damned young to retire."

It was a lie and they both knew it. Thirty-eight wasn't old by most standards, but in baseball it was damned near ancient. Before the injury, Angelo had remained a powerhouse, but his legs weren't what they used to be. Things like that didn't escape the notice of the guys in the dugout, much less the guys in management. This injury didn't help. It was his second serious one in three years, and pulled tendons had taken him out for several games in June. No ball club wanted to pay top dollar for a player who'd ride the pine. Even his agent was getting antsy that when Angelo's multimillion-dollar contract expired in a couple months the team would cut him loose.

"Well, it sounds like you'll have some time on your hands."

"Yeah." He studied the label on his beer and scraped at the edge with his thumbnail. "Maybe I'll mosey on down to Texas and pay you a visit. I could get better acquainted with your bride-to-be and her little girl."

It still came as a surprise that the pretty single mom had knocked his brooding brother off his feet when she'd shown up at the ranch with her disabled daughter a few months earlier. Alex wasn't the sort to fall fast or hard. Yet he'd done both.

"I'd like that." Alex paused then. "But what I'd like even more is for you to use the time to go to Italy."

Angelo closed his eyes. "Not this again," he muttered after an oath.

For weeks his twin had been urging on him to reconnect with their estranged father and meet the rest of the Casali clan in Monta Correnti, the place of their birth.

"Go and make your peace. You won't regret it," Alex said.

"I have no peace to make. I'm fine with things just the way they are."

"Fine? You're ticked off, Angelo."

"That too," he agreed after a long pull on his beer. "Where were they when we were stealing to eat or getting dumped into yet another foster home? Where was Luca?" he demanded, referring to their father. "No one was inviting us to Italy to visit then."

The way he saw it, the old man had washed his hands of his sons when he had sent them to Boston to live with their American mother, who was more suited to partying than parenting. They'd been three years old then. By the time the twins were fourteen, Cindy had drunk herself to death and the boys had been made wards of the state. Not long after, they'd made their way to New York. His skin still crawled when he thought about how close they'd come to winding up statistics.

"They didn't know, Angelo. None of them, including Luca, knew that Mom was gone or that we were in and out of the foster system."

"They didn't know because they didn't care enough to find out," he shot back.

In Angelo's mind, it was all very cut and dried. In the past, when it could have made a real difference, his family had wanted nothing to do with him. Well, he wanted nothing to do with them now, regardless of how many olive branches they extended.

He'd already ignored the surprise e-mail from his half-sister, Isabella, which had kicked off this whole reunion quest. Talk about a curveball. He certainly hadn't expected to learn via the Internet that he had additional siblings in Monta Correnti, three of them born to Luca's second wife after Angelo and Alex's exile. He'd also passed on a wedding invitation from a cousin who'd grown up in Australia.

Family had been falling out of the rafters for the past several months, but it was all too little and coming far too late.

"Don't think Luca doesn't regret his choices," Alex said quietly. "He does. But he can't go back and change the past. He can only try to change the future. Go to Italy, Angelo. Spend a week in Monta Correnti. In fact, spend two. You could use a vacation. I've already booked you a flight and found you a place to stay. I'll e-mail you the information. You can pay me back later."

"I'll drop a check in the mail first thing in the morning, bro. But I'm not going."

Alex was quiet a moment before he pulled out his ace. "If you won't do it for yourself, then do it for me. I'm asking you to go."

"That's low." And it was. His level-headed and older-by-mere-minutes brother knew he was the only person who could get Angelo to do something he didn't want to do.

Far from sounding insulted, Alex's voice held a smile when he replied, "Sure it's low, but it's also effective. You'll thank me later."

"Thank you? Right. Don't hold your breath," Angelo snapped before hanging up.

CHAPTER ONE

ATLANTA JACKSON expelled a gusty sigh as she studied herself in the hotel suite's full-length mirror. Was the pale, hollowed-eyed woman staring back really her?

The hair was right, a long cascade of nearly white-blonde curls. But her skin was pasty and her body a tad too angular to carry off the bombshell label that was routinely applied to it. She was a good half-dozen pounds thinner than she'd been just a month earlier, and ten pounds thinner than she'd been the month before that. Forget the low-carb fad that was all the rage among Hollywood A-listers. She'd gone on the high stress diet, guaranteed to melt off the pounds quicker than butter on Louisiana asphalt in August.

At least her dress, a simple navy sheath made of cotton, hid some of her new angles.

A smile bowed her lips. Zeke would hate this dress, which was precisely why she'd purchased it the day before at a pricy Fifth Avenue boutique, outside of which she had been mobbed by paparazzi and actually booed by a couple of passersby. Buying it and now wearing it out in public were acts of defiance.

Zeke Compton—her manager, mentor and, according to him, her messiah—hadn't allowed her to wear navy. It was too close to black, he claimed. Black being another forbidden color since it reminded him of mourning.

"What does America's favorite actress have to be sad about?" he'd asked the one time Atlanta's stylist had suggested a vintage Oscar de la Renta gown the color of onyx for a red-carpet event.

Wouldn't the public like to know? she'd thought at the time. Now she knew better. The public didn't want the truth, unvarnished or otherwise. They wanted romantic, rags-to-riches fairy tales and titillating scandals. They wouldn't accept that she was tired of being manipulated, tired of being dictated to and sick to death of living a lie.

Atlanta slipped on a pair of rounded-toe flats. Despite the fashionable little bow on them, the shoes were another no-no in Zeke's book.

"You're too short to wear anything less than a three-inch heel, love," he'd decreed one year into their professional relationship. By then, things between them also had turned personal, and she'd moved from her West Hollywood studio apartment into his Bellaire home, playing the dutiful Eliza Doolittle to his domineering Henry Higgins.

Atlanta was five-seven, hardly what one would consider petite, but she'd listened to him about clothing and shoes and pretty much everything else. She'd always listened to the men in her life, a habit that dated to her childhood.

Bad things happen to little girls who don't do what they're told.

The words echoed from her distant past. As she had done a million times before, Atlanta forced them and the black memories that accompanied them back. Then she glanced at her watch. It was time to go. Thank God, she thought, as she made her way out the suite's door. She was as eager to leave New York as she'd been to leave Los Angeles. Neither place was welcoming now that Zeke had poisoned the well of public opinion against her and made her a pariah among her peers.

In the elevator, she checked her purse one more time, making sure she had her itinerary, tickets and passport. Her luggage was waiting downstairs. The limousine she'd called for would be at the curb, only a gauntlet of paparazzi to run before she could relax in the relative privacy that its tinted windows would afford.

In a dozen hours she would be in Monta Correnti, Italy. Her stylist, one of the few people from her old life still willing to speak to her, assured Atlanta that the remote hillside village situated between Naples and Rome was the ideal place to drop off the radar, relax and rejuvenate.

God, she hoped Karen Somerville was right. Atlanta was wound so tightly these days she felt ready to explode. But first things first. Sucking in a deep breath, she donned a pair of dark designer sunglasses as the elevator's doors slid open.

"Show time," she murmured.

Eyes shaded with his trademark Oakleys, Angelo sauntered into the VIP lounge at JFK International as if he hadn't a care in the world. Image was everything, especially given all of the speculation swirling around his career.

The official line from the team was that Angelo was suffering pulled ligaments and severe tendonitis in his right shoulder, but that after rest and physical therapy he would return to the regular lineup in the spring. The truth wasn't quite as rosy as that. In addition to the start of osteoarthritis, he had a torn rotator cuff. Cortisone shots had kept the worst of the arthritis pain at bay in the past, but no shot would take care of the torn cuff.

As the team's physician bluntly put it, "You need surgery. An injury like this won't heal on its own. And, given your age, it might never heal well enough to take the abuse heaped on it by a major league ballplayer."

It all boiled down to a truth he wasn't ready to accept. Instead of scheduling surgery, he had embraced his brother's high-handed scheme for a family reunion. He was going to Italy, where he would spend the next couple of weeks. He had no intention of reconnecting with his father, but the gesture would appease Alex. As an added bonus, that little speck on the map was a good place to duck the press and figure out his future.

The bar area of the VIP lounge held only a smattering of patrons. None of them looked up when he entered. They were all important people in their own right—movers, shakers, captains of industry. They didn't get awestruck or if they did, they hid it well behind blasé attitudes. His ego certainly hoped that was the case with the gorgeous blonde sitting in front of the floor-to-ceiling window that overlooked the tarmac.

Despite the oversized sunglasses perched on her small nose, Atlanta Jackson was easy to recognize. The actress had starred in a dozen bona fide blockbusters. He took in the naturally pouty lips and the trademark blonde hair that tumbled just past her shoulders. Interest stirred. Again. He'd met her at a New York nightclub a few years earlier. They'd talked briefly. He'd flirted shamelessly, but to no avail. She'd turned him down flat when he'd asked her to dance. A couple of Angelo's teammates still liked to razz him about the fact that he, Angelo Casali, had struck out.

She shifted in her seat to cross her legs. The demure hemline of her simple navy dress pulled partway up her thighs. Interest turned to outright lust. Not many women were built as she was: long-limbed and slender, yet curvy in all of the places a man liked to rest his hands. A little less curvy than he recalled. He could guess why. Her image was taking a beating in the tabloids ever since she'd walked out on her much older manager slash boyfriend.

According to one story Angelo had read, the guy claimed Atlanta had betrayed him with a slew of lovers over the years, most recently bedding his twenty-year-old son.

Had she?

Maybe it was Angelo's ego talking, but the woman who'd turned him down flat in a nightclub a few years earlier hadn't seemed the sort to stray. With that in mind, he crossed to her table and waited until she looked up to speak.

"I'd offer to buy you a drink, but you'd probably turn me down. So, how about some meaningful conversation until one of our flights boards?"

He couldn't see her eyes behind the glasses, but her full lips twitched with amusement. "As lines go, that's very original, Mr. Casali."

"Thanks." He didn't wait to be offered a seat. He pulled out one of the chairs and straddled it backward. "So, you do remember me. I wasn't sure you would. It's been a few years."

His ego took another little hit when she replied, "Well, you've been in the news a lot these days."

"I could say the same about you."

Her mouth tightened fractionally. "Yes, I have."

"Is that why you're wearing sunglasses inside?"

"Maybe." She motioned to his Oakleys. "And you?"

"Definitely. This way no one can be sure I'm making eye contact with them. I find it discourages conversation."

A pair of finely arched brows rose over the top rim of her dark lenses.

"You find that ironic," he guessed.

"A little." She shrugged delicately.

"Here's the thing. Since you and I are the only two people in the lounge wearing shades I figure we probably should stick together. You know, play for the same team."

"Given all that is being said about me right now, are you sure you want me on your team, Mr. Casali?"

"The name is Angelo." He cocked his head to one side. "We'll consider this a tryout."

Atlanta laughed if for no other reason than the man's sheer nerve. A tryout? She hadn't had to read for a part in quite a while. The starring roles in her last three movies, each of which had grossed well over a hundred million dollars in the American market alone, had been written specifically with her in mind. Everyone in Hollywood knew that no one played the vulnerable vixen better than Atlanta Jackson. It was her niche. Her character type. She sobered at that.

"What if I don't want to be on your team?" she asked.

"You do."

She wanted to be turned off by his unflagging confidence or at the very least irritated by it. She found herself intrigued instead and maybe even a little envious. While she could portray confidence in front of the camera, she seldom felt it in real life. It was just one of the many things she was working to rectify.

"How can you be so sure?" she wanted to know.

"Everyone wants to be on the winning team."

"And that would be yours?"

"Of course. I've got the golden touch. The Rogues are in the playoffs because of me. We're heading to the World Series."

"That's only an assumption at this point."

"No. It's a fact, sweetheart. We'll be there."

Normally, she didn't care for empty endearments, but his casual use of sweetheart complemented his bravado so perfectly, she let it pass. Instead, she honed in on another matter.

"We? Are the news reports wrong, then?" Her gaze strayed to his shoulder. It didn't look injured. Indeed, nothing about the man's rock-hard physique appeared compromised...or compromising, for that matter.

"You know the media." He shrugged.

Atlanta might have believed that news of Angelo's professional demise was vastly overblown if he hadn't grimaced after making the casual movement.

"They're ruthless when they scent blood," he was saying.

Thinking of Zeke, she replied, "They're even more ruthless when they've got sources happy to help draw it."

Her image was being put through the shredder, and, while she wasn't all that sad to see some of the false layers she'd once agreed to peel away, she certainly didn't want them replaced with more lies and half-truths. Unfortunately, that was exactly what Zeke was feeding the hungry hordes these days, and they were eating it up, ravenous for more.

I made you. I'll ruin you.

Zeke's parting words. Foolishly, she hadn't believed he'd do it. She knew better now. He was doing a bang-up job of making good on his promise.

Angelo was apparently far less naïve than she. "The world is full of people eager to sell you out. You have to be careful who you trust."

"At this point, I trust no one." Surprised to have told him that, she asked, "Who do you trust?"

"My twin," he replied without hesitation. "Alex has always had my back."

"You have a twin?" Good heavens, there were two men on the planet as good-looking as this one? She'd worked with A-list actors, bona fide heartthrobs, who couldn't match Angelo's rugged male perfection. "Are you identical?"

"Not quite. I'm better looking."

"No doubt you're more modest, too," she replied dryly.

"Sure." Angelo wasn't put off. In fact, he pulled the sunglasses down the bridge of his nose and winked as he boasted, "I'm also better with women."

God help her. The man was every bit as sexy as she recalled from their brief meeting in a nightclub a few years back. He also was every bit as cocksure. She was used to being around oversized egos, her own included. Angelo, at least, tempered his with humor. He was harmless, she decided, especially here in a public place.

Which was what gave her the nerve to lean closer and say, "So, Don Juan, if I'm going to be on your team, perhaps you should explain the game we're playing."

"Distraction."

"Is that the name or the object?"

"Both."

"I'm intrigued. Tell me more."

He glanced at the chunky Rolex strapped to his wrist. "Here's the thing—I have an hour and forty minutes to kill before my flight departs. I could get my own table, order a drink and sip it alone while I wait. Or I could stay here with you and enjoy what is bound to be some fascinating conversation."

A lifetime ago, Atlanta had thought herself interesting, but it had been a very long time since a man had said so. "What makes you so sure the conversation would be fascinating?"

"You're a fascinating woman. What else would it be?"

Come-on or not, his reply caused her breath to catch. Clearly, being a pariah among the people she'd considered her friends had taken its toll on her self esteem.

"I like your answer," she told him.

"Enough to let me buy you a drink?"

"Enough that the drink's on me."

Angelo waved over a server and they ordered their beverages—an imported beer for him and a glass of unsweetened iced tea for her. As the waitress left he was frowning.

"Is something wrong?" she asked.

"Not wrong. I guess I thought you'd order something… else."

"Such as champagne perhaps? And not just any champagne but Piper-Heidsieck by the magnum?"

"Or Dom. I read once that you bathed in it."

"I read that, too."

"It's not true?"

She shook her head. "Afraid not."

"I'm disappointed. I was going to ask you what it felt

like having all of those bubbles bursting against your bare skin."

His smile, set as it was on a mouth that would have been at home on Michelangelo's David, dazzled. Atlanta camouflaged her involuntary shiver by shifting in her seat. There was no camouflaging the gooseflesh that pricked her arms. She hoped he wouldn't notice it.

"My publicist made that one up. It enjoyed a lot of buzz for a while, and I even picked up an endorsement deal for another brand of champagne. The truth is, I prefer showers to baths of any sort and I don't drink."

"At all?" he asked.

"Rarely these days." She preferred to keep a clear head.

"Neither do I."

"You just ordered a beer," she reminded him.

The corners of Angelo's mouth turned down as if in consideration and he gazed out the window where a jumbo jet was lumbering toward a runway. "Special circumstances."

"You don't like flying," she guessed. It was a phobia Atlanta understood perfectly. She still experienced a burst of anxiety each time a plane she was on prepared for takeoff.

But Angelo was shaking his head. "Nah. Flying doesn't bother me. I do it all the time. But talking to a gorgeous woman? It leaves me tongue-tied." Again, the dazzling smile made an appearance.

"I don't know. You've managed fine so far without any fortification," she pointed out, well aware that she could do with a little of the false courage found in a cocktail right about now herself.

Apropos of nothing, he asked, "When's your flight?"

"Two forty-something."

"Around the same time as mine, which means I've still got an hour and a half left with the potential to humiliate myself. I don't want to take any chances."

"I'm sure if we keep the conversation light and neutral, you'll be just fine."

And she would be just fine, too. So, that was precisely what they did.

It was with regret that Angelo glanced at his watch a little over an hour later. He would have to leave soon. It wasn't only the thought of what lay ahead in Italy that disturbed him. He couldn't remember the last time he'd had an actual conversation with a woman that didn't include foreplay of some sort or other. Both he and Atlanta still had their clothes on, a good thing given their surroundings. But they had ditched their sunglasses.

"If you didn't have a plane to catch, too, I'd hop on a later flight just so I could spend more time with you," he told her.

"Sure you would." She humored him with a smile, apparently deciding she'd just been fed another line.

"I mean it." He reached across the table and caught her left hand in his. Her fingers were delicate and bare of any adornment. "To be honest, I didn't expect to enjoy myself as much as I have."

Her brows pulled together at the same time she pulled her hand free. "Gee, thanks."

"Sorry." He grimaced. "That was a pathetically backhanded compliment. I told you I get tongue-tied around beautiful women."

The truth was the only beautiful woman around whom he'd ever found himself at a loss for words with was Atlanta.

Chuckling, she shook her head. "You're forgiven. I think I know what you mean. I enjoyed being distracted."

That was all he'd had in mind when he'd sat down earlier, someone to take his mind off the problems at hand. Now…?

"Maybe when we both get back to the States we could get together. If you're going to be in New York, there's a new exhibit coming to the Met in October."

"The Met?" Her eyelids flickered. No doubt she'd figured he was going to suggest a sporting event of some sort.

"I'm a patron."

"Oh."

"I'm not exactly the quote unquote dumb jock whose only interests are those that happen on the diamond."

"I didn't think you were. Honestly, I don't know you well enough to draw that conclusion."

"That doesn't stop most people."

She sighed. "Look, Angelo, I really appreciate the offer, but I've got a lot on my plate right now. Dating isn't going to be a priority for a while."

He nodded slowly, bemused and a little disappointed. "You know, that makes twice now that you've thrown me out before I got on base. Forgive me for saying so, Atlanta, but you're hell on a man's ego."

"I think you'll survive." She smiled. It wasn't the high-wattage sort the cameras captured. This one was the genuine article.

"Glad I could make your day," he grumbled.

"You did, Angelo, but not in the way you mean."

Atlanta rarely did anything spontaneous. Spontaneity was too costly. She'd found that out as a child. Under Zeke's care and later his control, she'd learned to deftly plan out her every move. She didn't plan to kiss Angelo Casali. She just leaned across the table and did it, resting her lips against his for a brief, sweet moment during which neither of them closed their eyes.

Innocent. That was what the gesture was. It had been a long time since she'd felt that way around a man, which was what caused her to draw away.

She gathered up her handbag and reached for her small carryon as she stood. Even though her legs felt ridiculously shaky, her voice came out steady. "From one wounded ego to another, thank you."

Atlanta stopped in the restroom after saying goodbye to Angelo. Taking several slow, measured breaths, she regained the last of her composure. Then, with her makeup freshened and her emotions firmly in check, she dropped the dark glasses back onto the bridge of her nose and hustled to the gate. She arrived just in time for the final boarding call for Flight 174 to Rome's Leonardo da Vinci International Airport. A flight attendant helped stow her carryon in one of the overhead compartments. Atlanta let out a sigh and turned to find her seat.

"Cutting it a little close, aren't you, sweetheart?" a masculine voice drawled.

Her neck snapped around and her gaze locked with Angelo's. He was two rows behind her on the opposite side of the aisle. So much for restoring her composure.

"Wh-what are you doing here?" she asked inanely.

He tugged at the strap of his seat belt. "Preparing for takeoff."

"Are…are you following me?"

She immediately felt like an idiot for making the assumption and that was before Angelo replied, "And you claim to have a wounded ego. Seems perfectly healthy to me."

Her gaze darted around. Thankfully none of the other passengers in first class seemed to be paying much attention.

"So, you're going to Italy," she managed on a weak smile.

"Yeah. Is that seat next to you open?"

Angelo didn't wait for her to reply. He unbuckled and rose, grinning as he plopped down beside her. One thought came through loud and clear: The flight to Italy was going to be interesting indeed.

CHAPTER TWO

"So, WHAT takes you to Italy?" Angelo asked once their flight was airborne. "A movie role?"

"A vacation, actually. I want some time alone without the media following my every move."

"So you picked a small town like Rome for that," he replied deadpan.

"Rome isn't my final destination." She lowered her voice. "I'm heading a little farther south to an isolated little village that I'd never heard of before. It's tucked up on a hillside, very remote and the people are very discreet when it comes to celebrities, or so I've been told."

No way, Angelo thought. What would be the odds? He had to know. "You're not talking about Monta Correnti, by any chance?"

"You know it?" Then her face paled. "You're...you're not going..."

"Yep." Angelo's laughter rang out loud enough to draw the attention of the passengers around them.

Distraction. In the airport's VIP lounge he'd told Atlanta it was the name of their game as well as its object. Apparently they were going into extra innings.

A couple hours into their flight, Angelo could no longer ignore the angry throbbing of his shoulder.

Atlanta was reading a magazine, or more likely pretending to since she hadn't turned the page in twenty minutes. He was no speed-reader, but even he could have finished the article on eyeliner dos and don'ts in that amount of time.

He twisted the cap off the mineral water he'd ordered when the flight attendant last came around, and as discreetly as possible popped a couple of the potent painkillers the team doctor had prescribed, washing them down with a gulp of the beverage.

"That bad, huh?" She closed the magazine and laid it on her lap.

"Just stiff," he lied. "I'll be all right." He had to be.

After the pills kicked in, he didn't wake until shortly before the aircraft was making its final descent into the larger of Rome's two airports. He was hungry, having slept through the dinner that was served during the flight, the medicine was wearing off and his overall mood wasn't much improved.

Through the thick glass of the plane's window, Angelo caught his first glimpse of Italy in thirty-five years. Even with the floral scent of Atlanta's perfume teasing his senses, he could no longer ignore his real reason for coming.

"Sleep well?" she asked.

"Like a baby."

"You moaned a few times. I thought maybe you were in pain."

"Erotic dreams," he corrected on a wink.

"My mistake." But she rolled her eyes.

"Sir, your seat needs to be in the upright position," a flight attendant stopped by to remind him.

He shifted and a moan escaped before he could muffle it.

"Apparently you have those dreams even when you're awake," Atlanta said dryly.

"Want me to share the particulars with you?"

"That's all right."

"Sure? I wouldn't mind."

"I'm sure you wouldn't, but I'll pass."

"How long are you going to be staying in Monta—?"

"Shh!" she admonished and glanced around as if she expected to find the other first class passengers shamelessly eavesdropping. That was a virtual impossibility over the loud hum of the jet engines. Still, he obliged her by lowering his voice.

"So, how long?"

Her eyes narrowed. "Why?"

"Just curious how much time I'll have to wear you down. Eventually, even though you claim not to drink, I predict you and I will share a bottle of wine and some more fascinating conversation."

She chuckled. "What do you call this?"

"You're avoiding answering my question."

"Fine. I'll be there for three glorious weeks with an option to stay four." She sighed, as eager to arrive as he was to have the trip behind him.

"I'll be there two weeks tops. Might as well be a life sentence," he mumbled.

"Excuse me?"

"Nothing. You never said what made you decide to make Monta—" he caught himself before he finished the village's name "—MC your final destination. It's a speck on the map, you know."

If she heard the derision in his tone, she didn't comment on it. "That's why it's ideal."

"Ah, that's right. Hiding out."

A line formed between her brows. "That makes me sound like a coward."

"Sorry. I didn't—"

"No." She waved off the rest of his apology. "I guess I am hiding out. I just needed a place to go to recharge my batteries." Her expression turned rueful. "Someplace where I wouldn't have to deal with booing fans or the paparazzi at every turn. My stylist suggested the village. She visited it a few years ago. She was seeing a rather famous actor at the time and according to her they could go anywhere in town without worrying about drawing a crowd, much less paparazzi."

Frowning, Angelo said, "It's nothing like LA or New York, that's for sure."

"So, this isn't your first visit?"

He shook his head.

"What's it like?"

"It's been a while, years in fact."

Vague images of quaint, red-tile-roofed houses tucked into the side of a hill rose from his memory, accompanied by the scents of fresh basil, roasted red peppers and plum tomatoes. Angelo couldn't be sure if they were real or the result of wishful thinking. As it was, nothing of his childhood in Boston evoked anything worth recalling.

"I looked it up on Google," Atlanta was saying. "There's not a lot of information, but I did find some photographs. It's very picturesque and old-fashioned, like a snapshot out of the past."

His past.

Her gaze shifted to his shoulder. Her expression held understanding. "Are you interested in dropping out of sight for a while, too?"

"Not exactly." He took a deep breath before admitting, "My father lives there."

Atlanta blinked, not quite able to hide her surprise.

"Yes, I have one of those," he replied dryly.

"From the scowl on your face I gather the two of you aren't close."

"I haven't seen him in thirty-five years." And Angelo had no desire to see Luca now.

"Ouch. Sorry."

He laughed outright as a cover for the pain he couldn't admit to feeling. "It's no big deal. I didn't need him and I haven't missed him. Hell, I barely remember him."

"So, why are you going? If you don't mind me asking," she added.

He shrugged. The pain the gesture caused made him wince. "My brother booked my flight and my accommodations. Alex thinks that making peace with our father is important."

"But you don't share his opinion," she guessed.

Angelo caught himself before he could shrug again. "It's ancient history. What's to be gained?"

"I'm the wrong person to ask," Atlanta admitted. "I haven't seen my mother in years. My choice."

"You're smart. The only reason my brother is all for a reunion now is that he's met a woman and they're getting married. He's *in love*."

"From your tone I'd take it you're not a big fan of the emotion."

"I've got nothing against love. I'm happy for my brother."

How could Angelo not be? Allie, the woman Alex was marrying, was pretty, kind and intelligent. She had a daughter whom his brother obviously adored. Together they were a ready-made family. If that thought made him feel unbearably alone at times, it was his own problem. He'd get over it.

"Have you ever been in love yourself?" Atlanta asked.

"You're a regular Oprah. So many questions," he teased, stretching out his stiff legs. He hoped whatever accommodations Alex had arranged came with a jetted tub. He could do with a nice long soak.

"Sorry." She ruined the apology by adding, "Well?"

"No. I like women in general too much to commit to any one in particular." He sent Atlanta a wolfish smile that caused her to roll her sky-blue eyes.

"Gee, that's romantic," she said dryly.

"No, that's realistic. I could say something cliché like I haven't met the right woman, but I don't think the right woman exists."

"Your brother apparently disagrees."

Angelo held up a finger. "Let me clarify. I don't believe the right woman exists *for me*." It was a long-held belief, one that predated puberty. Commitment? His parents had gone that route and look how it had turned out. They hadn't been able to keep the promises they made to one another, let alone to the children they'd brought into the world. He grinned wickedly to banish the old bitterness, hiding behind the cockiness that was as much his trademark as Atlanta's bombshell looks were hers. "But if she did exist, she'd be blonde, about your height and have ridiculously long legs."

Atlanta crossed her arms and sent him a pointed look. "Do lines like that actually work for you?"

"Apparently not," he replied with feigned disappointment.

She shook her head. "You're incorrigible."

"I know. A judge told me that very thing before

sending me off to juvie when I was a kid." He said it lightly, though nothing about the incident could be considered fun or funny. Before she could comment he said, "I won't bother to ask if you've ever been in love. You lived with that Zeke guy for—what?—a decade?"

"Something like that," she murmured. Her gaze strayed to the window.

"But no ring?" he prodded.

"Not the kind you're talking about."

Curious, he asked, "What other kind is there?"

It sounded as if she said, "Through the nose," but he couldn't be sure.

"I find it hard to believe he didn't propose. If I were the sort of guy interested in lifelong commitments, I'd have been on bended knee after our first date."

Atlanta made a tsking noise. "Obviously you're not up on your tabloid reports. Zeke proposed dozens of times during the course of our relationship. Actually, begged is how I believe he put it. He wanted to marry me. He wanted to have a family with me. Heartless witch that I am, I repeatedly turned him down. I didn't want a husband and I didn't want babies. My figure is my fortune, you know. I'm nothing without a twenty-four-inch waist and flawless abs."

He'd seen pictures of the abs in question. Still, he said, "You sell yourself short."

She glanced over sharply, studied him for a moment. It might have been a trick of the light, but her eyes looked bright. "It doesn't really matter now."

The captain came on the public address system announcing the local time and temperature and the usual end-of-the-flight banter. Afterward, Angelo asked, "Should I apologize for prying?"

A ghost of a smile tugged at the corners of her mouth.

Even without her usual crimson gloss, her lips were full and inviting. "Are you sorry?"

Since she was striving to remain upbeat, he decided to oblige her. "No. I'm too curious to be sorry. You're quite an enigma."

"Me?" She laughed. "Everybody knows everything there is to know about me."

Did they? People thought they knew him, too. Since his injury, Angelo had begun to wonder if he knew himself.

Alex had assured Angelo that a driver would be waiting to take him to Monta Correnti. A rental car would be at his disposal in the village, but his brother figured Angelo would appreciate having someone else navigate the roads after a long flight. Alex had thought of everything, perhaps so that Angelo wouldn't have any excuses for backing out.

Atlanta had someone meeting her as well. Even so, they stayed together after deplaning.

"Want me to help you with your bags?" she asked.

"That's supposed to be my line."

She tilted her head to one side. "I'm not the one with a bum shoulder."

"It's fine," he protested through gritted teeth.

Her brows rose but she said nothing else as they waited to spot their bags on the conveyor belt. One by one, Atlanta's four pieces of matching designer luggage came around before Angelo's large suitcase. She snatched them off before he could offer.

"I thought you said you were going to be in Italy for less than a month?" he drawled as a bushy-haired porter hurried over with a cart. "From the amount of luggage, it looks like you're planning to move here."

"I like clothes and shoes."

"That's obvious. You could outfit the population of a small country."

She wrinkled her nose. "Sorry. I'm incredibly selfish when it comes to my shoes. I don't share."

"How many pairs did you bring?"

"Twelve, not counting the ones I'm wearing." She looked inordinately pleased when she announced, "Almost all of them have heels less than one inch."

"No stilettos?"

"Not a one."

"Damn." He spied his bag and moved closer to the conveyor to snatch it. She was at his side in an instant, helping him heft the bulky suitcase off.

"I've got it," he grumbled.

"Of course you do, big he-man that you are. You don't need anybody."

Angelo laughed, even if in truth he didn't want to need anybody. He'd learned a long time ago to rely on himself. The only people he trusted to help him out when needed were his twin and, of course, his teammates.

Assuming they were together, the bushy-haired porter added Angelo's bag to the cart stacked with Atlanta's.

"We're going to owe him a really big tip when it's all said and done," Angelo muttered as the man started off toward Customs.

"It's not like we can't afford it."

No indeed. She was one of the few women he'd ever met who actually made as much money as he did, perhaps more, since he didn't know what her cut had been on her past few movies.

Still, he had enough pride that he said, "I'll get this one since you picked up the tab in the lounge."

"Grazie mille," she said, batting her lashes at him for effect.

After they cleared Customs, she dropped the sunglasses back onto the bridge of her nose. Before landing, she'd pulled her hair back into a simple ponytail. Along with the navy dress and flat-heeled shoes, she hardly screamed high-maintenance Hollywood. But such raw beauty rarely went unnoticed. As low-key as she was trying to be, as soon as they passed into the main terminal she attracted a lot of attention and some of it was exactly the kind she wanted to avoid.

A couple of photographers began shouting her name. Even prefaced with the courtesy title of Signorina the intrusion was rude, especially since it was followed by a succession of near-blinding flashes. Atlanta held up her handbag as a shield. Just that quickly, the witty and surprisingly candid woman with whom he'd spent the past several hours was swallowed up by a monster of her own making.

Fame. Sometimes it grew fangs and bit you.

Angelo waited for the photographers to holler out his name, too. It was their lucky day. The parasites had a pair of American celebrities in their viewfinders. He patted his pockets in search of his Oakleys. He was as used to dealing with them as Atlanta was. On any given day, half a dozen of their ilk stood guard outside his Manhattan apartment building, their digital cameras trained on the exits in the hope of snapping a money shot or two for the tabloids.

"I'm going to duck into the ladies' room for a minute," Atlanta whispered. "You go on ahead to your car. Tell the porter to wait there with my bags."

"Divide and conquer?" he asked.

"Maybe we'll get lucky."

"See you in MC."

She didn't answer. They'd reached the ladies' room and she hustled inside.

Angelo turned. He'd found his sunglasses but needn't have bothered. With Atlanta gone, the paparazzi lowered their cameras. It came as a huge blow to realize that he hadn't been recognized. Baseball was a largely American game, he reminded himself. Neither it nor its players resonated much outside the United States, and apparently that was true in Italy.

He should have been relieved. It was a pain to be hounded by the paparazzi. Even so, he felt sucker-punched. Was this what his life would be like post-career? Would no one recognize him? Would no one care that for four consecutive seasons he'd led the league in runs batted in or that he was half a dozen homers from passing the current record? Would he return to the obscurity from which he'd come, a mere postscript in write-ups about the game that had literally saved his life?

The porter nudged him and said something in Italian. It was Angelo's native tongue, but he remembered none of it even if he found the accent and cadence oddly comforting.

"Sorry. I only speak English," he replied.

"Taxi?" the man said helpfully and pointed to an overhead sign designating the way to ground transportation.

"Ah, no. Someone is meeting me."

Several of those waiting to welcome passengers were holding signs with names written on them. One was printed with Angelo's. "My driver."

"Signorina?" The porter glanced back to the restroom door.

She had her own transportation. She'd told Angelo to go. Yet Angelo told the porter, "We'll wait for her here."

He knew the moment she was out in the open. The paparazzi descended on her like a pack of wolves on prey. Long legs and irritation made her pace fast, but eventually, she had nowhere left to run.

"I told you to leave," she snapped, turning this way and that in an effort to avoid the cameras.

Angelo stood perfectly still. "I'm bad at following directions. It's a guy thing."

"This will make a fine headline."

"They don't know who I am."

"They will back home. You'll be labeled as my latest conquest."

"Yeah?"

"Don't look so smug," she cried. "That's not a good thing."

"From your point of view," he replied, hoping to see her smile.

Her expression remained grim.

"You need to get out of here," he told her.

"I would, but apparently my driver is late." Her laughter verged on hysteria.

"It's Italy," Angelo said. "I've been told they run on their own time here."

More camera flashes popped. Atlanta backed up, trying to put as much distance between herself and Angelo in the photographers' frames as possible.

"Come with me. We're heading to the same place."

He extended a hand. She declined both it and his offer with a shake of her head. "No, no. That's kind, but I have my own transportation. Or I will. Soon."

The photographers snapped off a couple more shots.

In addition to paparazzi they were drawing a crowd of onlookers, some of whom had pulled out their camera phones. Within a matter of hours this was going to be all over the Internet.

"Do you really want to wait around?" he asked.

"I…" She issued a heartfelt sigh. "God, no."

Along with the porter and driver, they made a mad dash for the exit. At the curb, Angelo peeled off some bills, trying to remember the exchange rate of dollars to euros. At the porter's broad grin, he figured the tip was as generous as intended.

He grinned, too, but for an entirely different reason.

CHAPTER THREE

ATLANTA assumed that the closer they drew to Monta Correnti and the villa she'd rented, the more relaxed she would feel. But just the opposite was occurring, probably because the small, isolated village was Angelo's final destination, too.

While it was entirely likely they would bump into each other a time or two during the next couple weeks, she didn't want it to become a habit. She was enjoying his company...a little too much. She found him funny and surprisingly interesting. He was far more than the inflated ego and one-dimensional jock she'd first assumed. She also found him intensely attractive. Their kiss kept coming to mind. It had her yearning for something she'd lost long ago. Something she could never get back.

It was just as well this wasn't a true vacation for either of them. He was in Italy to meet with his estranged father. She had come to escape the media's prying eyes. She had a career to save, a reputation to salvage. A life to start over without the guiding influence of a man. Any man. By the time the driver pulled the Mercedes sedan to a stop outside a sun-bleached two-story villa, she had rehearsed the lines in her head for her farewell speech.

"Great view," Angelo remarked before she could get the first words out.

The pre-World-War-II residence was bounded on one side by a cobblestone courtyard, part of which was shaded by a grapevine-draped pergola. Beyond it, the land sloped gently down before falling away completely to reveal a valley dotted with houses, farms and olive groves.

"Stunning," she agreed. "Well, thank you again. I hope you enjoy your stay here."

She reached for the door handle, intent on making her exit. Angelo ruined it by following her out.

"From what Alex has told me about the place I'm staying, it has an equally gorgeous view. It's farther up the hillside. If you want to stop by tomorrow evening, we can compare panoramas before going to dinner."

The invitation was delivered so smoothly that she nearly agreed. "I appreciate the offer, but I think I'll be eating in for most of my stay."

The driver had retrieved her bags from the trunk. Despite her objections, Angelo insisted on carrying one of them to the door. After the man returned to the car to wait, Angelo said, "I thought one of the reasons in coming to Monta Correnti was the discretion of the locals. Does that scene at the airport have you worried about being ambushed by paparazzi?"

"No. I just need time alone…to reflect and make plans. You understand, right?"

Angelo whistled through his teeth. "I can't believe I just struck out for the third time with you. You'd think I'd learn." The accompanying smile took the sting out of his words. Even so, Atlanta felt bad.

"I'm sorry. It's not you personally. In fact, I was just

thinking about how much I've enjoyed your company on the trip here. It's bad timing."

"For dinner?"

"You know what I mean."

"No." He set his hands on his hips. "Not really. I'm talking about a meal."

She changed tactics. "You're talking about avoidance, as in avoiding the real reason you came here. Your father."

"My choice. My business." His expression lost some of its easy charm, telling her she'd struck a nerve. So much for his earlier claim not to care about the estrangement. But the affable smile was back when he said, "What's the harm, Atlanta? We've already established that I'm not interested in a long-term relationship and you're not ready for one. What's wrong with a little... friendship?"

He stepped closer and ran his knuckles lightly down her cheek, making it clear he had more than friendship in mind. God help her, the simple touch stoked her pulse to life. Her feelings scared her almost as much as what he was suggesting. "We're two Americans in a foreign country. What happens here stays here."

He wound up his tempting offer with, "No one needs to ever find out."

Don't tell your mother. It's our little secret.

Bile rose in her throat, along with anger and a baffling amount of disappointment. But she kept her tone even when she said, "Let me put this another way: I'm not interested in continuing as your distraction, Angelo."

Indeed. She'd spent too many years being just that: A sick father figure's plaything. A powerful man's puppet.

Angelo frowned. "You just said you're not looking for strings."

"I'm not, but while I didn't mind being a distraction during the trip over, that scenario has played out." She took a step back. "To use your vernacular, the game is over."

He sucked in a breath and stepped back with his palms up in defeat. "Got it, sweetheart. Enjoy your stay."

She watched the Mercedes drive away. Should she have been so blunt? Could she have handled things differently, more diplomatically, perhaps? Though she was beset with doubts and some regret, one thing came through clearly. As angry and irritated as Angelo had been, he'd respected her decision.

As she stood on the steps replaying the encounter, the door behind her opened. A young woman stood just inside the entry. She wore a plain cotton dress and her dark hair was parted in the middle and pulled back.

"Miss Jackson, welcome," she said in heavily accented English. "I am Franca Bruno."

The name registered as Atlanta stepped inside. This was the owner of the house. "Thank you. I was just admiring the view. My travel agent said it was lovely and he wasn't mistaken."

The woman glanced at the bags before poking her head out the door. "Is my husband with you? He was supposed to pick you up from the airport."

"No. I caught another ride."

Franca's dark eyes narrowed and she rattled off something in Italian that didn't sound particularly nice. "He was late, wasn't he?"

"Maybe just a little," Atlanta hedged, not wanting to get in the middle of a domestic dispute. "Unfortunately, circumstances came up that forced me to leave in a rush. I was lucky to run into a friend who also was coming to Monta Correnti."

That snagged Franca's attention. "Another American?"

"Yes. Angelo Casali."

Franca nodded. "Luca's other son. I had heard that he might come. I am pleased for his father's sake that it is so. Signor Casali is a kind man…and far more reliable than my husband."

Franca helped Atlanta pull her bags inside. "Come, let me show you around."

In addition to the stunning view, the villa boasted three large bedrooms, three bathrooms, formal sitting and dining rooms, and what appeared to be a study. The furnishings were an eclectic mix of charming old-world pieces and modern conveniences such as the flat-screen television that hung over the fireplace in the study and the microwave oven that sat on the counter opposite a brick pizza oven.

Atlanta had everything she needed. Franca had stocked the refrigerator with food and had even gone to the trouble of preparing an antipasto salad in case Atlanta was too jet-lagged to go out later that evening.

"You will find bottled water and local vintage red wine in the pantry. I am happy to prepare any meals you request."

"Thank you. The antipasto will hold me over for tonight."

Together they walked back to the door and Atlanta followed the other woman outside.

"I hope you will enjoy your stay."

"I'll be hard-pressed not to." She spread out her hands to encompass the scenery. "It's truly lovely here."

"It is a special place," Franca agreed. "It belonged to my grandparents. My husband and I live just down the hill. I will be by each morning to freshen up the linens and take care of anything else you need."

After Franca was gone, Atlanta headed upstairs. The only thing she needed right now was a hot shower and a few hours of uninterrupted sleep. Unlike Angelo, she'd spent the entire flight wide awake and way too aware of not only the sexy man slumbering next to her, but her physical response to him.

The game is over.

Angelo mulled Atlanta's parting words on the way to his villa. He wanted to be able to shrug them off... shrug her off. There were plenty of other fish in the sea. He knew that firsthand. So, why did he feel so damned disappointed? Maybe because at times while they'd talked, it hadn't felt like a game.

It was the painkillers, he decided as the driver turned off the main road and passed through a gated drive. They made his brain fuzzy.

A turn-of-the-last-century villa came into sight. Its view of the surrounding countryside was worth every penny of the rent. His courtyard sported more than the cobblestones and grapevines that graced Atlanta's. His had a built-in pool and spa.

While the driver took his bags inside, Angelo walked over to inspect the amenities. The pool wasn't Olympic size, but he wasn't in any condition to swim laps anyway. The hot tub was more his speed, he thought on a grin. He could picture himself in it, the pulsating jets working the tension out of his muscles as he enjoyed a glass of red wine and watched the sun set. If he had to stay in Monta Correnti, at least he would be comfortable.

From what he'd seen so far, his brother had done well in choosing accommodations. He headed back to the house.

Alex hadn't said anything about meals being included, but when Angelo stepped inside he was greeted by the mouth-watering aroma of garlic, onions and assorted herbs. He inhaled deeply, letting the scents linger in his nose. Snippets of memories came to him before he could stop them, popping like corn kernels held over a flame. He recalled following his father to a nearby riverbed to pick the special basil that Luca said gave his tomato sauce its distinctive flavor. Alex was with them. Angelo swallowed now, remembering how happy the boys had been and how he'd basked in their father's attention. It was not long after that that Luca sent his sons away.

"No wonder I've never been a fan of spaghetti," he muttered with a shake of his head.

"Actually, I am making ravioli stuffed with portabella mushrooms and roasted garlic." A young woman stood on the opposite side of the room. Given her apron and her words, he assumed the door from which she'd entered must be the kitchen. She was dark-haired and lovely with surprisingly blue eyes. Eyes that were the exact shade of his, a trait he had inherited from his father.

"Isabella," he guessed, feeling mule-kicked.

So this was the sister he'd never met and had only learned about recently. Yet another reason to resent Luca. But it wasn't only resentment he felt. Emotions Angelo couldn't label, much less process, raced through his head. For so long he'd just had Alex. Now he was meeting a sister, and Luca had two other sons who shared the Casali name, as well.

Clearly, Isabella had more practice in handling the

surreal. While he stood gaping, she smiled warmly at the mention of her name.

"And you are Angelo." She crossed to him and rose up on tiptoe to kiss both of his cheeks. It was a standard Italian greeting, he reminded himself when a lump rose in his throat. "Welcome home."

"This…this is Luca's home?" He glanced around. Other than the aroma wafting from the kitchen, nothing about the place was remotely familiar.

"No. I meant welcome to Monta Correnti," Isabella clarified. "An American businessman owns this particular villa. He leases it out when he is not here, which is most of the time. Alessandro said he thought it would suit your needs."

Angelo nodded. Unsure what else to say, he told her, "Your English is very good."

"Better than your Italian?" Isabella's smile told him she already knew the answer to her question.

"It could use some work."

"So could your brother's when I met him. But he learned a lot during the time he was here." Her satisfied expression made Angelo think she was referring to more than the language. "Alessandro is a good man. I was grateful that he came, and I am even more grateful that he was able to convince you to come as well."

Angelo needed to set the record straight. "I'm not sure the outcome of my visit will be what you're hoping for, Isabella. Alex and I may look a lot alike, but that doesn't mean we think the same."

She took a moment to weigh his words before nodding. "You are here. That is enough for now. We will see about the rest later." She wiped her hands on her apron, a gesture that spoke of nerves more than necessity. "Come. You must be tired after your long journey. I can show you around."

"Actually, I'm not all that tired. I slept most of the way." He hated that he still felt a little groggy from the medication. Despite the returning pain, he was determined to forgo another dose. He had too much to process to be lost in the fog.

"Are you hungry, then?" Isabella asked.

He hadn't been since leaving the plane. Between the visit to come and Atlanta's intoxicating company, he'd been way too keyed up to think about food. Now, his empty stomach made its presence known with a loud growl, which she heard.

"I guess I am," he said sheepishly.

Isabella smiled, clearly pleased. "I was hoping that would be the case. I will set the table while you freshen up. You will find a bathroom down there." She pointed to a hallway that led from the room. "It's the first door on the right. You will find a larger one upstairs. Your rooms are on the second floor to the left of the landing."

Angelo opted for the former. A few minutes later, after splashing a little water on his face and adjusting his wrinkled clothes, he joined Isabella in the kitchen. Even though the villa had a formal dining room appointed with intricately carved mahogany furnishings, she'd set the wooden-plank table in what was a surprisingly plain kitchen. Plain and downright rustic, he thought, glancing around.

"I hope you don't mind," she said. "The other room is fancier, but so big and formal. We are family."

The word was as foreign to him as her accent. "I take it the American businessman who owns this place isn't much of a chef."

"No. On the rare occasions when he is here, he takes all of his meals in the village. But you are not to worry," she said, as if reading Angelo's mind. "You will find the master suite very comfortable. He has done what you would call extensive updating elsewhere in the house."

"And outside as well. It was kind of hard to miss the in-ground pool and hot tub."

"They look very inviting," Isabella agreed.

"So does this meal."

She motioned with her arms. "Then sit and enjoy."

While he lowered himself into one of the chairs, she filled his glass with red wine. He tried not to stare, but he couldn't help it. When she glanced up and caught him, they both flushed.

"I'm sorry. It's just...disturbing, you know?" When her brows pulled together in puzzlement, he added, "Seeing a resemblance in a stranger's face."

"The eyes."

"Yes, and our chins." At her startled expression, he laughed. "Don't worry. Yours is much smaller and far more refined."

"And this resemblance disturbs you?"

He decided to be frank. "For most of my life, it's been just Alex and me."

"But your mother— "

"Even then," he interrupted. Given Cindy's fair looks and her absorption with partying, it had been easy to discount her role in their lives. As for Luca, whenever Angelo had thought of their father, he hadn't considered the possibility of half-siblings. Or maybe he simply had been unable to process the idea that Luca could send away his twins and then someday have children he would keep. Confused and a great deal more curious than he wanted to be, he said, "You know, I'm a big eater, but there's enough here to feed a small army."

"I cook when I'm nervous," she admitted on a laugh.

"Why don't you join me and enjoy some of the fruits of your labor?"

A smile lit her face. "I would like that." As she took the seat opposite his it was obvious she knew the real reason he'd issued the invitation. "It will give us a chance to get better acquainted with one another."

He wasn't exaggerating about the amount of food. In addition to the pasta dish, which she'd served with the savory tomato sauce that had assaulted his senses upon arrival, the table included a loaf of thick-crusted bread, steamed green beans and a side of some sort of sausage that she told him was produced locally.

"This is excellent," he declared after his first bite of ravioli. It was no empty compliment. The flavors sang in his mouth. "You're an excellent cook."

"I cannot take all of the credit. The sauce is the real star."

"It's very good." In fact, he'd never tasted its equal, which made his aversion to bottled pasta sauce all the more understandable.

"It's very popular with our patrons."

"At Rosa." Despite his best effort, the name was hissed between clenched teeth. From Alex, Angelo had heard a lot about the quaint and rustic eatery their father owned and had named for their late grandmother. Far from taking pride in it, he saw the place as competition. After all, it was what Luca had squandered his time, love and attention on after shipping his sons off to America.

"I used to spend more time there than I did away,"

Isabella mused. Shook her head and laughed. "Scarlett, our cousin from Australia, manages it now. Her husband to be, Lorenzo, is the chef. But I am still there a lot."

"Why do you bother? Why do any of you bother to slave away for him?"

She sobered. "I have a full life, Angelo. As does Scarlett. I am married to a wonderful man and very happy. I work for our father because I enjoy what I do."

Angelo snorted. "You must to put up with him."

"That's unfair," Isabella objected. "You know nothing of Luca."

"Only because that's the way he wanted it," he shot back. "From what Alex has told me, the restaurant isn't doing as well as it could be these days. Money is tight."

Her face had paled. "That is true. He insists on using local produce and labor, and sometimes that has cost him more than if he'd outsourced."

The anger that had been simmering for the better part of three decades rolled to a boil. "So, call in the millionaire stepbrother to help save the day."

Isabella's cheeks flamed red now and she shot to her feet. She shouted something in Italian before she collected herself and, in a more moderated tone, replied in English, "I will apologize if that is the way it seems, but what you are saying is not true. Money is not why I sought out either you or Alex and asked you to come to Monta Correnti."

He wanted to believe her. Even so, he challenged, "Then why? Why now?"

"I only recently learned of your existence, Angelo."

He crossed his arms over his chest. "That makes

two of us. Again, Luca's choice. Or, should I say, his fault?"

He had her there and she knew it. But Isabella raised that small chin that was so similar to his.

"My motives for asking you to come here are very simple. I have two older brothers whom I wished to meet and a rift in our family that I wish to see mended. These are the reasons I sought Luca's permission to contact you and Alex in America." She unknotted her fingers from the cloth napkin she held and set it on the table. "If all I needed was money to save Rosa, Angelo, my husband would be happy to provide it. It is not beyond his means, and he has generously offered to do so on more than one occasion."

"But you've turned him down."

"Yes. *Family* is more important than the restaurant, but *family* is what it will take to save it."

She needn't have stressed the word. It would have struck him like a prizefighter's blow anyway. He'd never viewed family as the sort of savior she was implying it could be. Before he could respond, she was going on.

"We have a plan in mind. Our cousins and I. We want to combine our families' restaurants. They are joined by a courtyard. It is time they were joined in other ways."

"How does Luca feel about that?"

"He knows nothing of the plan. We want to surprise him. We want everyone who is descended from our grandmother, Rosa Firenzi, to come together. As I said, it will take all of us to make it happen."

He didn't question whether she was referring to funding now. He knew better.

Isabella rose to her feet. "I will leave you now to

finish your meal and to settle in. I have things I must see to."

"At the restaurant?" It was a low blow and he knew it. Shame stirred, making him wish it were possible to snatch back the words and start over.

Instead of answering his question, Isabella said, "If you want for anything, I wrote my number next to the telephone in the front parlor."

With that, his sister disappeared out the door. Angelo stood so abruptly that his chair tipped backward, clattering noisily on the tiled floor. He wanted to call her back so he could apologize. He felt horrible, putting her on the defensive, especially when she'd gone to such trouble to make his first day in Monta Correnti pleasant.

Besides, this wasn't her fault. None of it was. Luca was the one responsible for the rift in their family. Their father was the one who had screwed up all of their lives with his selfishness and single-minded pursuits.

Oh, Alex had tried to palm off some of the blame on Lisa Firenzi, Luca's older sister and the owner of the restaurant with which Isabella wanted to join Rosa. According to Angelo, if only their aunt had given Luca the loan he'd sought when the boys were toddlers, they could have remained in Italy rather than being sent to live with Cindy. Angelo wasn't buying it. Ultimately, the choice had been Luca's.

Angelo didn't go after his sister. Instead, he uncorked the bottle of wine and filled his glass to the rim. Then, without bothering to change into the swim trunks that were packed in the luggage the driver had toted upstairs, he went outside and lowered himself fully clothed into the hot tub.

It would be several hours yet before the sun set,

but, lost as he was in bitter memories of his fractured childhood, he really didn't give a damn about either his pricey clothes or the million-dollar view.

CHAPTER FOUR

ANGELO woke early the next morning with a pounding headache that was the result of jet lag, regrets and too much wine. He'd finished off the bottle the evening before. In fact, he'd sat in the hot tub drinking it. Now, not quite dawn, he was in his bed. His head was throbbing more than his shoulder, but not quite as much as his conscience.

He owed Isabella an apology.

Women. This made two who'd gotten under his skin in short order in ways that he hadn't thought possible.

Last night, after a second glass of wine and half an hour of bubbling hot water had mellowed his mood, he'd considered going to see Atlanta. He'd poured himself more *vino* and brooded instead. He'd never pursued a woman in the past. He'd never needed to. Yet he found himself practically chasing Atlanta and eager to see her even though she'd made it clear she wanted solitude. And that she didn't want him. He didn't care for the fact he was acting like some lovesick teen.

As for Isabella, his sister had welcomed him to Monta Correnti with a feast suitable for a returning prodigal son, which in a way he guessed he was. They were strangers, yet they also were siblings. Half, whole or otherwise, she hadn't felt the need to sever their kinship.

She'd made it clear all she wanted was a chance to get to know her long-lost brother. A chance to right a wrong and mend a rift. In return, all she asked of Angelo was for him to keep an open mind when it came to their father and the rest of the family.

He'd blown that deal before they'd finished eating the pasta she'd no doubt spent hours preparing. God, he was a heel. He had to make amends. He waited until it was a reasonable hour and called the number she'd left, only to find out she wasn't home.

The man who answered the phone told Angelo in heavily accented English that she was in the village running errands and he didn't expect her back for a couple hours.

"This is Angelo, no?" the man asked gruffly.

Guilty as charged, he thought. "Yes."

"I am Max, Isabella's husband."

Not sure what else to say, Angelo replied, "It's nice to meet you."

Max didn't bother with inane pleasantries. "Isabella was upset when she returned to our home last night."

"That would be my fault."

"*Sì.* She told me as much. You made her very angry." Max's voice softened when he added, "My Isabella is especially pretty when her temper flares."

Angelo had heard that tone before. His brother used it whenever the subject of his intended came up.

Max was saying, "As much as it was my pleasure to take her mind off family matters, it is my duty to look out for her well-being. I do not wish to see her distraught again."

Under other circumstances, the man's subtle threat might have irritated Angelo. In this case, he figured he deserved it. Besides, he'd already managed to get off on a bad foot with relatives. No sense making matters worse by getting into a verbal boxing match with Max.

So, he said, "Neither do I. In fact, that's why I'm calling. I'd hoped to apologize to her. I knew even before she left that I was way out of line."

"Good." Max sounded pleased. "If you happen to be in the village this afternoon, you can find her at Rosa."

And chance running into Luca? No, thanks, Angelo thought.

Max seemed to read his mind. "Your father will not be at the restaurant today. In fact, he is away from Monta Correnti on a buying trip to the coast for fresh seafood. He prefers to take care of important business in person."

Max's message was clear. Angelo should offer his apology to Isabella in person as well.

He was right, too, Angelo thought after ending the call. Hadn't Big Mike, the only foster father he'd ever considered worthy of the title, taught Angelo that very lesson right along with tips for how to steal a base when the pitcher wasn't looking?

Dressed and ready to eat whatever amount of crow was necessary, he started off for the village a little later. He figured he could poke around a bit before going to see Isabella.

In New York or while on the road with his team, Angelo left the driving to others. Here, he had a car at his disposal, a sporty little five-speed that his brother had thoughtfully rented on his behalf. He was itching to get behind the wheel, but he decided to walk. He could use the fresh air and exercise. Besides, he was too off-kilter to remember which side of the road he was supposed to be on.

The temperature was cool when he started out, the air still moist from dew. After a while, the sun poked through the filmy layer of clouds. Between its warmth and Angelo's physical exertion, by the time he reached the village he was regretting the jacket he'd pulled over his button-down shirt. He shrugged it off and slung it over his good shoulder as he made his way down cobbled streets that looked like something straight out of Brigadoon.

He navigated his way around what he figured was the main business district. With each turn, he discovered quaint shops and encountered the homey smells of fresh-baked bread and drying herbs. Based on his reaction the previous day to scent, he waited for some blast of recognition or sense of déjà vu to slow his steps. But while he definitely found Monta Correnti inviting and the smells mouthwatering, none of it was familiar.

Angelo told himself he was relieved. The last thing he wanted at the moment was to take a trip down memory lane. So what if the place of his birth didn't ring any mental bells? Why would it? He'd barely spent three years here. He and Alex had spent more than a decade with their apathetic mother in a Boston apartment building, and those memories were good and buried. That was how he preferred it. As far as he was concerned, his life had begun the day a scout from a small private college in upstate New York had come knocking at his foster family's door. It hadn't been the big leagues, but it had helped pave the way to them.

Lost in good memories, he took a moment to recognize the woman who emerged from the pastry shop at the corner. It was Atlanta.

She was wearing jeans, the faded boot-cut variety, and a ridiculously prim apple-green sweater set that did nothing to diminish her sex appeal. She might as well have been outfitted in skin-tight leather pants and a low-cut leopard-print blouse given the way his body reacted.

She's not interested, he reminded himself. She'd made that abundantly clear. He was just starting to turn in the opposite direction when she spied him and offered a tentative wave. He waved back and though he intended that to be the end of the encounter, his feet had other ideas. They started off in her direction.

"Good morning," he said when he reached her.

"Buongiorno."

"Show off. You listened to Berlitz tapes before you came," he accused, finding it easier to distance himself from real emotions by hiding behind teasing humor.

For her part, Atlanta looked almost relieved.

"Actually, I had to learn a little Italian for a movie I did a few years back. I liked the language, so I brushed up on it before traveling." As she spoke, she tucked the little white pastry bag behind her back.

"What have you got in there?" he asked, craning to one side.

"N-nothing." She looked and sounded nervous. Not nervous, he amended. Guilty. But he'd be damned if he could figure out why.

"Did you knock over the pastry shop or something?"

Her mouth fell open and she sputtered a moment before finally managing a full sentence. "Why on earth would you say that?"

"Because you're acting suspicious." He retrieved the bag from her hands. "It's like you've got the Hope diamond stuffed in there or something."

She snatched it away before he could open it. "It's just a cannolo."

"A cannolo?" All that subterfuge for a damned pastry? He said as much.

She sighed. "Okay, two. I couldn't resist. They were fresh-made this morning."

"Mmm. Nothing like a freshly made cannolo." Angelo's mouth watered a little, but it wasn't the pastry alone that had whetted his appetite. "Were you planning to share with someone?"

"No. I bought them for me." She laughed and some of her nervousness leaked away. "I guess that's why I seemed so guilty. I can't believe I bought one cannolo, much less two and just for myself."

"What's so wrong with that?"

"I planned to eat them both. In one sitting." The last part was confessed in a near whisper with her gaze glued to the tips of her shoes.

"Is that a crime?"

"Yes." She shook her head then and her gaze reconnected with his. "No. Of course not. Unless you're Darnell."

"Darnell?"

"My sadistic personal trainer. Since I've been away from Los Angeles he's text-messaged me nearly every day to ask if I've been working out and sticking to my diet."

Though he knew he'd regret it, Angelo allowed his gaze to slip south. The woman had a killer body. It was perfectly proportioned, even if parts of it were a little less full these days. "I don't think you need to worry about a diet right now."

"I've lost a little weight," she admitted. "I call it the stress diet." She touched a finger to her chin, the pose intentionally thoughtful. "You know, maybe I should patent it and start hawking it to young starlets as a backup plan in case my career never recovers."

"That would be a waste of your talent. Besides, I like women with some curves."

"Some curves." She nodded. "But there's a fine line, which is why Zeke wouldn't let me…"

She flushed and didn't finish, but Angelo figured he could fill in the blanks easily enough. It sounded as if the guy had done a real number on her. Let it go, he told himself. Leave it alone. He had enough problems of his own to concentrate on without taking on Atlanta's, especially since she'd made it abundantly plain she was not interested in sharing a cannolo or anything else with him.

He hitched one thumb over his shoulder and took a step backward. "I should be going."

"Yes. I should, too."

"You wouldn't want those cannoli to get stale." He motioned toward the bag as he backed up another step.

"No." She forced out a laugh. "It was nice seeing you, Angelo."

He stopped. "Was it?"

His point-blank question caused her to blink. "I…I feel bad about yesterday. About…about how things ended between us."

"Well, as you said, it was time for them to end. The game was over and all," he drawled.

Atlanta winced. "That came out…"

"Wrong?" He shook his head. "I don't think so. Actually, I appreciate your honesty."

She blinked again, this time looking more piqued than perplexed. "I doubt that. You were clearly mad."

Royally ticked was more like it. But he smiled now. "Whatever. Water under the bridge."

"Then why bring it up?"

"I didn't."

"You did."

Damn. She had him there. He glanced past her up the block. A coffee shop caught his attention. He told himself it was only the promise of his first cup of java that caused him to say, "I want a cannolo."

"What?"

"A cannolo. I'll buy the espresso if you'll share your cannoli. It doesn't even have to be a whole one. I'll settle for a bite or two."

Her eyes narrowed. "You want a cannolo?"

"That's what I said." He held his breath, half expecting her to state the obvious and tell him to go buy his own.

Instead, to his surprise, she said slowly, "I guess that's a reasonable trade."

The coffee shop was small with limited seating inside and only half a dozen wrought-iron tables and chairs on its speck of a cobblestone patio. Most of the tables indoors were unoccupied, but it was too nice a day to sit inside. Outdoors, only two were empty. They took a seat at one of them and waited for the server to come for their order. Angelo went with espresso, the stronger the better in his opinion, especially given the rough start to his day. Atlanta opted for a cappuccino.

"In for a penny, in for a pound," she announced when their beverages arrived.

"What do you mean by that?" he asked.

She pointed to the rich froth that topped her cup. "This is steamed whole milk and the espresso isn't decaffeinated. Do you have any idea how long it's been since I allowed myself to have either?" She didn't wait for Angelo to answer. "And a cannolo!" She pulled one of the pastries in question from the paper bag. "I would be eating two if you hadn't talked me into being nice and sharing."

She tried to hand him one of the tempting pastries, but he refused to take it. "I've changed my mind. I want you to eat them both. And I want to watch."

"God, no! Please, Angelo. Save me from myself." Though the drama of her words was definitely for effect, he sensed a nugget of truth—and perhaps of fear—in them.

He leaned back in his chair. "What's to save, sweetheart? Everyone's entitled to a little indulgence from time to time."

Still eyeing the cannolo, she nodded. "I know."

"Do you?"

"Some habits are hard to break," she said softly.

"Zeke?"

She set the cannolo on a napkin and glanced away. "You think it's stupid that I let a man run my life to such a degree for so long."

"Is that what I think? Or is that what you think?" he asked, reneging on his earlier promise to himself to stay out of her business. He'd also vowed to steer clear of her. As the woman said, in for a penny, in for a pound.

"It's what I think."

"So, how'd it happen?"

Her brow furrowed. "It wasn't all at once. I thought I was free…"

"Free?"

She cleared her throat. "You know. Footloose and fancy free. God knows, I was all attitude when I first arrived in Hollywood. I didn't look in the rearview mirror when I left rural Louisiana. I was happy to kiss my hick roots and…and everything else goodbye."

The way she hesitated made him think there was more to it than that, but he commented on the obvious. "I thought you were born in Georgia?"

One side of her mouth rose. "That's what you're supposed to think. It was Zeke's idea after he came up with my name. Atlanta is one of his favorite cities, very cosmopolitan but with a bit of edge. He said it suited me."

"What is your given name?"

"Jane. Jane Marie Lutz."

It was a nice enough name, but it didn't fit her, Angelo decided as he took in the tumble of nearly white hair and the blue eyes that, even without the benefit of much makeup, were her face's star feature.

"Forgive me for saying so, but you don't look like a Jane."

Her laughter held little humor. "Zeke's words exactly. He wanted something exotic, something people would remember. A name that could be used all by itself and people would know who you meant."

"Like Cher or Madonna."

She nodded. "You got it. The idea of being that famous caught my attention, even if at first I wasn't too excited about being called Atlanta. Still, I was willing to do whatever Zeke suggested. He was a Hollywood big shot who had managed the careers of some of the hottest names in the business, and I was a nobody who wanted to be a star. I was grateful to him, pathetically so, for believing that I could be."

"I don't think he had to overtax his imagination. He

must have seen a spark of something that he knew would have broad appeal."

"He saw my body," she said dryly. "I was nineteen, wearing a G-string and pasties and performing onstage at a gentleman's club. Not my finest hour and definitely not the career I envisioned when I traded in my Podunk Ville address for a cockroach-invested walkup in Tinsel Town."

A G-string and pasties.

Angelo had too much testosterone not to hone in on those words and be turned on by the erotic image they evoked. Somehow, however, he managed to say in a remarkably normal tone, "It takes more than a hot body and pretty face to become a mainstay in Hollywood. Lots of actresses with only that to recommend them have come and gone, while you've remained a box-office draw. You're selling yourself short again."

He expected her to argue, but she didn't. Neither did she agree. Instead, she tore open a white packet of sugar and added it to her beverage. Another act of defiance, he was sure.

"So what does all of this have to do with a couple of cannoli and caffeine laced with whole milk and now some sugar?" he asked.

"Zeke was strict about what I could eat." She exhaled and shook her head. "And about what I could drink, wear...you name it."

"Controlling?"

"He claimed that he was only looking out for my best interests."

Of course he did.

"Controlling," Angelo said again, this time not as a question but as a statement.

"He was right about a lot of things, though. He got

me my first big break. I didn't want the part of Daisy Maddox." It was the role that had made her a bona fide star. "He insisted I take it and it wound up being my best-grossing movie."

"Are you defending him?" Angelo asked.

"No." She looked insulted. "I'm merely pointing out the hand he had in making my career."

"So, you're defending him."

"No!"

"He could have had the same impact on your career without treating you like a lump of clay to be molded to his exact specifications."

She shook her head. "You don't understand."

"Do you?"

"He managed what has been a very successful career for me."

"So, that meant he got to manage your life, too?"

"Of course not."

"As for your career, is it all you envisioned for yourself?"

He wasn't sure what made him ask the question, but he was glad he had when he saw her mouth drop open. "I...I have other ideas, other avenues I'd like to explore."

"Let me guess. He didn't want you to explore them."

Her gaze slid away. "Let's drop it."

"Sure."

Atlanta grew quiet. He considered apologizing, but he wasn't really sorry. She'd been under the guy's thumb for way too long. Angelo didn't want to see her slip beneath it again, even for a moment. No one deserved that kind of treatment.

She dipped the tip of her index finger into the custard

that oozed from the end of the cannolo and licked it off. All thoughts of Zeke vanished. In fact, thoughts of every variety except the lustful kind vanished. It was all he could do not to groan.

"That's a good start. But you can do better."

When she looked at him in question, he nodded to the cannolo.

She dipped her finger in a second time for another nibble. He snagged her wrist before she could and brought it to his mouth instead, taking his time licking off the last of the rich filling. The quick intake of her breath was all of the encouragement he needed.

"I know all about indulgence, Atlanta. You might say I'm an expert."

She pulled her fingers free and reached for her cappuccino. The hands holding the cup weren't completely steady. He knew the feeling.

"Seduced in Italy."

"Excuse me?" She gaped at him and his ego needed to believe she looked every bit as guilty as she had over the cannoli.

"The name of the movie you learned Italian for."

"Oh. Right." She smiled. "That was the one. It was shot on location in Venice. I loved it there."

"Was Zeke with you?"

"Only for the first couple days, then he had to fly back to LA for business."

"Perhaps that's why you enjoyed Venice so much. It's a city known for indulgence."

She shrugged, non-committal, and took another sip of her cappuccino. "I'm guessing you were on a date when you saw the movie."

"Why do you say that?"

"It's a chick flick. I can't see you going with a couple of guys from the team."

"You're right." His expression was unrepentant when he said, "I don't remember the woman I was with, but I remember the scene where you danced in the fountain in that really sheer top."

"What a surprise," Atlanta replied dryly.

Angelo was flirting with her again, although at times it seemed as if he was testing himself as much as her. Either way, flirting was harmless, she decided. Come to that, even though she'd had precious little practice at it away from the big screen, it was all but required when two healthy and unattached adults got together in an idyllic setting. In Angelo's case, it was second nature and indicative of nothing more than his interest in a romp in the sack. The man had a one-track mind.

He needn't bother. She was the polar opposite of her celluloid twin, the recent stirrings of her libido not-withstanding. With a crew looking on and a camera recording her every move and emotion, she'd enticed and seduced her leading man or fallen victim to his charms. In real life, however, she'd always been care-ful not to send out signals or offer come-hither glances and coy smiles. She considered that to be too close to her mother's method of operation when it came to men. Too close to what her stepfather had accused Atlanta of doing to assuage his conscience for the petting and pawing that had begun even before she'd hit puberty.

Even with Zeke, Atlanta had felt awkward and had approached sex with a straightforwardness that had siphoned off every last ounce of romance from the act. He hadn't seemed to mind, which she realized now was because for him romance had never entered into it.

"Is something wrong with your dessert?" Angelo's question roused her from her thoughts.

"No. It's fine. Delicious, in fact." She reached for her napkin and blotted the corners of her mouth.

"Then why are you frowning?"

"I wasn't aware that I was."

"You are."

"If I am, it's not the company." She said it automatically. She'd had a lot of practice placating men.

"Sure it is." Angelo's eyes narrowed. "I make you nervous."

"Please." She waved a hand. "What do I have to be nervous about?"

"You're attracted to me."

She huffed out an impatient breath to camouflage the truth. "Right. And that would make me nervous?"

"Yeah," he said slowly. "You're not as confident in real life as you are in your movies."

So, he'd figured that out, had he? Well, points to him.

"That's because I'm a person, not a character for whom every action and reaction has been scripted." She crossed her arms. "You, on the other hand, come across as grossly overconfident."

"It's not overconfidence if you can back it up with actions."

"I'm talking off the ball diamond."

"So am I."

"Is that so, *sweetheart*?" she drawled. "I hate to tell you this, but, all of your bravado aside, you're no more certain of yourself than I am. It's easy to flirt and throw out pickup lines, but you've admitted that you aren't capable of cultivating a real relationship."

"I didn't say I was incapable." The calf that had been

rubbing against hers under the table stilled. "I said it's not what I want."

"Uh-huh. The right woman doesn't exist for you. I remember the conversation. Have you ever *had* a relationship? And I'm talking about something that involves more than the exchange of apartment keys and regular sex."

A muscle twitched in his jaw. "As I said, that's not what I want."

"Why?" It was her turn to play therapist, and if it kept her out of the hot seat, all the better. "Is your life so perfect flying solo all the time?"

"That's right."

"No. That's what you want everybody to think. Most people buy it. I don't. What insecurities are you trying to mask? Hmm? What are your secrets?"

He shifted back in his chair, his gaze turning guarded. She'd struck a nerve.

"You know, I almost turned around and walked the other way when I saw you today," he admitted.

"Regretting that you didn't?"

He didn't answer.

"You don't like it when the shoe is on the other foot," she said.

"It's damned uncomfortable," he surprised her by admitting.

"Then maybe you'll resist the next time you're tempted to analyze me."

"Maybe. I probably should." He shrugged. "For that matter, I should probably leave you alone entirely. You've asked me to. I don't usually pursue a woman who tells me not to bother."

"Then why are you?"

She expected him to mention attraction again. What he said was, "I can't quite figure you out, Atlanta."

Her laughter was bitter. "No one else seems to have a problem."

"Yeah, I thought I had, too. But you're a bundle of contradictions. Strong one moment, vulnerable the next."

She shifted uncomfortably in her seat. "Maybe I'm both. Maybe I'm neither. I am an actress."

"Uh-uh. My turn to tell you I'm not buying it. This is you. Not an act. Contradictions," he said again. "Like the way you keep telling me no but—"

That was as far as he got. She shot to her feet, rapping her hip against the edge of the table and spilling both of their beverages.

"When I say no, I mean no."

"Atlanta."

"No means no!"

He reached out a hand in entreaty, but she shook her head, turned and fled.

CHAPTER FIVE

What was that all about?

Alone at the café, Angelo slumped back in his chair and replayed the encounter. Atlanta had surprised him twice. First, by turning the tables on him and questioning what his secrets and vulnerabilities might be. And then with her overreaction to his admittedly poor choice of words.

He was a firm believer that when a woman said no, she meant no, but that was in the bedroom. He hadn't been talking about sex, at least not directly; although where Atlanta was concerned, it was much on his mind.

"I should have walked the other way," he muttered.

He didn't have time to sort through her emotional baggage. As she'd already figured out, he had enough of his own.

Standing, he tossed some bills onto the table alongside her discarded cannoli and left to meander through the town. He had a little more time to kill before seeing Isabella.

Everyone he passed in Monta Correnti was friendly. From the shop owners to their customers to the people milling about on the streets, they smiled and called out polite greetings. But not one of them asked for Angelo's autograph. Not one of them asked him to stop and pose for a photograph. Almost absently, he rubbed his shoulder. Just as he had at the airport in Rome, he found anonymity disturbing. He also found his need for fame disturbing.

What insecurities are you hiding? Atlanta had asked.

"Buongiorno."

He glanced up to find a young woman standing beside a pushcart of freshly cut flowers. The blooms were separated by kind and color and tucked into individual buckets of water. The overall effect was lovely, as was the cart's owner. He guessed her to be in her mid-twenties. She had a ripe figure, Sophia Loren eyes and mahogany-colored hair that tumbled halfway down her back.

"Hi, uh, *buongiorno.*"

She switched to English when she asked, "Do you see something you like, *signor?*"

The invitation in her smile was unmistakable, as was his appalling lack of interest. Here was the kind of mindless distraction he needed, yet the thought of spending time with her—clothed or otherwise—held virtually no appeal. Now, if she'd had blonde hair and blue eyes... He glanced past her to the cart.

"Um, how about some roses?"

"Roses." Her disappointment was clear.

"A dozen white." The perfect peace offering for his sister, he decided.

The woman gathered the blooms and added some greenery to the arrangement. Her movements were deft but her enthusiasm to make a sale had waned considerably. That much was all the more obvious when she thrust the bouquet into his hands and spat out a price.

He was reaching into his pocket for his wallet when a burly older man rushed over shouting something in Italian. The words were directed at the young woman, who cast Angelo a second appraising look before leaving.

"You are Luca's son, no?"

Despite the label's uncomfortable fit, Angelo answered, "Yes, um, *sì*."

"I am Andrea. I own the village floral shop. My daughter, Bianca, looks after the cart for me. I provide flowers for the tables at Rosa." He cast another dark look in her direction before continuing. "Luca, he is so good to me and my family. He is good to many of us in Monta Correnti. So, I give you these flowers for half the price."

Angelo fought the ridiculous urge to argue. Instead he offered a stilted, *"Grazie."*

After twenty minutes of brooding and walking, he arrived at his father's restaurant. The exterior of Rosa was just as his brother described it, a rustic stone façade with arched windows. Directly next to it was the more upscale eatery Sorella. Their aunt, Luca's older sister Lisa, owned it. The two restaurants shared a wall and a gated courtyard, but otherwise they had little in common.

According to Alex, Sorella's cuisine was contemporary and international, the sort of stuff that could be found at the trendy restaurants of New York. That sounded more like Angelo's kind of thing. A peek through the restaurant's wide windows revealed a stylish interior that leaned toward modern with its chrome and glass fixtures and sleek furnishings.

Definitely more my thing, he thought. The designer he'd hired a couple years back to make over his

Manhattan apartment had done the rooms in a similar style.

Both restaurants were open for business. Rosa's door was propped open. Music drifted from inside, something classical and soothing that probably was written around the same time the building was erected. Angelo stepped through the door and was immediately welcomed by the aroma of freshly baked bread and the same tomato sauce Isabella had made for him the evening before. His stomach growled.

A young woman stood at the hostess station. She smiled politely and offered a greeting.

"Ciao," he replied. "I'm Angelo Casali." His name, he figured, would say it all.

Based on the way her face lit up, it did. *"Sì,sì.* Yes. Welcome. Signor Casali is not here."

Which was exactly why Angelo was willing to set foot in the place today. He smiled.

"Actually, I was hoping to see Isabella. Her husband told me I might find her here."

"Isabella. *Sì.* She is taking a telephone call right now, but I will tell her you are here. Have a seat." The young woman pointed to a table near the front window that offered a view of the street. "Can I get you a cup of espresso to drink while you wait?"

The thought of more caffeine on an empty stomach held zero appeal. "Just water, please."

She returned a moment later with a bottle of sparkling water and a glass.

"Isabella said to tell you she will be with you soon. Also, your cousin Scarlett is in her office. Shall I get her for you?"

"No. That's all right. I don't want to disturb her."

He was bound to meet all of the Casali clan before

he returned to New York, but he wasn't in the mood to do it now. The young woman nodded and left him to greet a group of tourists that had just come through the door.

Though it was barely a quarter past noon, Rosa was already filling up with patrons. The place was popular, no doubt about it. He figured the rich aromas that had greeted him when he stepped through the door explained why. He'd come here on a mission. He didn't want to be hungry. Nor did he want to feel this odd sense of pride. But he did.

Someone arrived with a basket of warm bread. When he glanced up to offer his thanks, he saw that it was Isabella.

"Angelo. Hello. I hope you are well rested." The words were offered with a polite if restrained smile. His doing, he knew.

"Yes," he lied, even though nothing about the previous night had been restful.

"I wasn't expecting to see you here today. Luca is away."

"I know."

Her smile was sad. "Of course, you do."

Angelo decided to cut to the chase. "I came because I owe you an apology and I didn't want to let it wait."

Isabella's brows rose, but she said nothing. He took that as a positive sign and reached over to pull out the chair next to his. When she was seated he continued.

"I offended you yesterday, and for that I'm sorry. You were nothing but kind, fixing me a meal and making me feel welcome on my first day in Monta Correnti, and I was rude."

A smile, this one more genuine than polite, creased her cheeks. "Yes, you were."

Her teasing reply, as much as her impish expression, made it easy to accept they really were siblings. "Unforgivably so?" he asked.

"Never, especially if those flowers are for me."

He'd nearly forgotten about the roses. He picked up the bouquet now and handed it to her. "I thought it was a fitting gesture."

"And very sweet. I cannot remember our other brothers ever giving me such a peace offering. When we were little, Cristiano and Valentino used to tickle me till I forgave them." As she buried her face in the blooms Angelo almost could hear the echoes of childish laughter. It unsettled him because he regretted not having been a part of it. She smiled at him. "I think I like your act of contrition better."

"I'm just glad you're no longer upset with me."

"How could I be?" She set the roses aside and clasped his hands firmly in her much smaller ones. "We're family, Angelo."

He didn't argue, even though the concept still seemed so foreign. But he needed to make one thing clear. "I don't know that I can forgive him, Isabella. What Luca did, it's not the same as a surly mood. Sorry and flowers won't fix it."

She sobered slightly as she settled back in her chair. "I only ask that, when you are ready, you will listen to what he has to say."

Angelo nodded and sipped his water. Still, he had to know. "Why is it so important to you?"

She seemed perplexed by the question. "We are family, Angelo. *Familia*. What is more important than that?"

He envied Isabella's passion on the subject. This made twice in a matter of minutes that she'd referenced their shared bloodline. He wanted to be swayed by her argument, to get behind it with as much conviction. Even with half as much. But the truth was, "The only family I've had for a very long time is Alex."

Her gaze held compassion as well as empathy. "I understand from your brother that your mother died when you were teenagers."

"She drank herself to death," he said bluntly. "Cindy…" An embarrassing rush of emotions washed away the rest of his words. He shook his head and tried again. "She was never going to win any Mother of the Year awards, you know? But she was all we had."

"My mamma is gone as well. She died when I was young." Her gaze softened. "I still miss her."

Alex had mentioned that Luca's second wife, Violetta, had been killed in a tragic fall. Fate could be crueler than addiction, even though some might argue that it didn't matter since the end result was the same. But fate put things outside one's control. "That's rough. Sorry."

"I remember her a little, as does Valentino. He is the youngest. Cristiano, who is two years older than I am, has more memories." Her expression clouded.

"I get the feeling that even though you weren't the oldest, you took care of them." What little he knew of Isabella pointed to a take-charge person. After all, she'd been the one to initiate contact with Angelo and Alex. The peacemaker, the bridge-maker. He'd admire the characteristics more if they weren't running against his own goals.

"I did."

"And you helped out here." He made a circular motion with one hand.

"Yes. Our father was lost in his grief after Mamma died. He needed me."

Luca and his needs. It took all of Angelo's willpower not to sneer.

"Why aren't you bitter?" He hadn't intended to ask that question, so he shook his head. "Never mind. I came here to apologize to you, not to pick another fight."

"I will answer anyway. Bitterness serves no useful purpose, Angelo. I would have liked a different childhood, *sì*. One with fewer cares and responsibilities, but…" Isabella's shoulders rose.

"Well, you're obviously happy now."

"I am. Very." Blue eyes that were so like his own lit with an emotion that Angelo had yet to experience for himself.

"Alex said you're married, and to a real prince, no less."

Her smile grew wider. "Maximilliano Di Rossi."

"I spoke to him today. He wasn't very happy with me."

Her laughter was pleased and wholly female. "He can be very protective."

"So I gathered."

"You will meet him and some of the others at the—" Isabella broke off and blushed.

"At the what?"

"Party."

"Let me guess. I'm to be the guest of honor," he said dryly.

She wrinkled her nose. "Would you rather not have such a gathering? If that is your wish I can call the others and explain. They can meet with you individually during the course of your stay in Italy."

Now there was an even less appealing thought. Better

to get it over with in one fell swoop than prolong the agony over days. "No. A party is fine. When is it and where?"

"We thought we would give you a chance to settle in first, get to know some people. So it is planned for a week from Friday at eight o'clock. Our plan is to close Rosa early for the occasion. Valentino will be here. Cristiano, unfortunately, can't be. He's a firefighter and was injured during a blaze in Rome."

A strange feeling of concern stirred for this stranger who shared his bloodline. "Is he…okay?"

Isabella's smile was all-knowing. "He will be." Then, "You are sure a family party is all right with you?"

"Yes."

Her expression turned wily when she mentioned, "You could bring someone."

"Who would I bring?" he asked, though he had the feeling his sister had someone in mind.

She did. "How about Atlanta Jackson? I have heard from no fewer than three sources already this morning that you were spotted sharing cannoli with the pretty actress at the café up the street."

And Atlanta's abrupt departure? Had they mentioned that?

"Is everything all right, Angelo?"

"Fine. It's just that she came here hoping to get away. She doesn't want to draw any attention to herself."

"Nor will she," Isabella assured him. "The villagers are curious about her, but they will leave her be. No one will ask for autographs or pictures. The wealthy and famous come here because they know they can count on our discretion. In turn, they keep our economy going."

"Good. She's going through a rough patch professionally and personally. The last thing she needs right now is to find herself being tailed by the media, legitimate or otherwise."

"I have read some of the things her ex is saying."

"Lies." But Angelo didn't think Zeke's cruelty or control were the only demons she needed to exorcise.

Isabella tilted her head to one side. "You seem very… concerned about her. Have you and this Atlanta known one another for very long?"

"We don't really know one another at all," he said slowly.

His sister smiled before helpfully suggesting, "Perhaps you can remedy that while you are here."

Atlanta rubbed her throbbing forehead with one hand and pressed the telephone to her ear with the other as Sara Daniels, one of the few true friends she had in Los Angeles, confirmed her worst fears.

"I hate to tell you this, but you're still making headlines. When I stopped for coffee on my way into work this morning, I saw pictures of you and Angelo Casali together in Rome's airport on the front page of a couple of tabloids."

Even as she bit back a groan Atlanta forced herself to ask, "What are they saying about me now?"

"Hon, you don't want to know."

"No, I don't, but tell me anyway." Forewarned was forearmed.

Sara heaved a sigh. "Okay. The headline on the one in *The Scoop* is, um, 'Angel and the Tramp'. The article claims that the two of you have been involved on and off for years."

"Of course it does. And the other tabloid? What did it come up with for a headline?"

"Keep in mind the writer is probably a Rogues fan, okay?" Sara hedged.

"Okay." Atlanta's forehead throbbed more insistently.

"'New York's Angel falls under Hollywood seductress's spell.'"

This time Atlanta wasn't able to hold back her groan. Glutton for punishment that she was, she asked, "What does it say?"

"The usual tripe about how Angelo is another of your many conquests. It includes a quote from Zeke. He, um, says he feels sorry for Mr. Casali and is a little surprised you went after him considering that the ballplayer is past his prime and not likely to continue in the spotlight much longer, unless, given his recent injury, it's to do endorsements for over-the-counter pain medicine."

"God, he's a piece of work," she spat, insulted on Angelo's behalf. "If he wants to trash me, fine. But he has no right to drag anyone else into the mud."

"Speaking of Angelo, how exactly did the two of you hook up?"

"We haven't *hooked up*. We were on the same flight, headed to the same place and he was kind enough to share his car with me after I was spotted by those photographers."

"So, that was the end of it?"

"We bumped into each other again today." She swallowed, thinking of how she'd overreacted during their conversation. And she had overreacted. She could see that now.

"Do you plan to see each other again?"

After her earlier display? He probably thought her to be either the quintessential drama queen or a complete nut. Either way, it was for the best. He had her thinking things, remembering things, best left alone.

It's not your fault.

A therapist had assured her of that, although it hadn't been necessary. Atlanta had always known who to blame. Her stepfather. Duke had been an adult and a parental figure. She'd been but a frightened girl who'd had the misfortune to blossom early and live in a trailer with a man who believed he was entitled to do as he pleased and a mother who chose to look the other way because she was too afraid of being alone.

No means no.

Knowing that didn't automatically make everything all right, though.

Thankfully, acting out a love scene in front of a camera had never been much of a problem for her, perhaps because she knew exactly what to expect. She knew when it would start and when it would stop. She knew what her reactions were supposed to be. The one time a co-star had tried to ad lib a bit too much for her liking, she'd ended the scene and walked off the set. Being in control made it easier, it made it almost cathartic, and it helped to block out the bad memories. Still, she considered it a testament to her acting ability that she could make the world believe she was truly enjoying herself.

As an adult, it had taken a long time for Atlanta to actually have sex without getting physically sick afterward. After a decade with Zeke, she'd gotten to the point where she sometimes could enjoy herself, though she rarely wound up fully satisfied. She was fine with that. Or she had been…until recently. Angelo had her wondering what she might have been missing.

"Atlanta?" Sara's voice brought her back to the present.

"What?"

"I asked if you were going to see him again."

"No," she replied with conviction.

"Hmm. Too bad."

"Why do you say that?"

Sara's laughter came over the line. "Have you gone blind or taken vows with a religious order since you've been gone?"

"My vision is perfect and, no, I doubt I'll ever be a candidate for the abbey."

"Well, then, if you tell me that man isn't every bit as sexy in real life as he comes across on television, I'm going to be crushed."

Atlanta nearly shivered as she recalled the way Angelo had licked cannolo custard from her fingers. "It's no trick of the cameras. He's sexy, all right."

"I thought so."

To counteract her friend's smugness, Atlanta said, "And so is every male co-star I've worked with during my career. It doesn't mean I want to sleep with them."

"Who said anything about sleeping together?" Sara asked. "I merely asked if you were going to see him again."

"My answer hasn't changed. No."

"You could do a lot worse."

"Sara."

"Just saying. I mean, it's not like I could see the two of you together for the long haul. But for a vacation fling? A post-Zeke fling?" Her friend sighed dreamily. "He's perfect."

"I'm not here for a fling," Atlanta replied impatiently, but Sara was right about one thing: if she were the sort of woman who engaged in casual, no-strings encounters, Angelo would be perfect.

For the better part of the afternoon, Atlanta hung around the villa going through the stack of scripts she'd brought with her. None was written by an established name. That was half of their appeal. The parts hadn't been penned with her in mind. They didn't play to her known strengths, mainly her sex appeal. She would have to adapt herself to these parts, in some cases change physically to do the characters justice.

Cut and dye her trademark locks? Gain a dozen pounds? The very idea was scary but exciting, too. Zeke never would have allowed it, but how else would she ever prove herself as more than a sex symbol?

You sell yourself short.

Angelo had told her that twice now.

She set a script in her lap. Angelo. He was so different from Zeke. She didn't mean to compare the men, but it was impossible not to. Physically, they were night and day. Zeke was lean with an elegant build. He claimed to be six feet tall, but she suspected he was closer to five ten. He also claimed to be fifty-two, but she knew for a fact that he was fifty-seven. He looked good for his age, though, thanks to regular workouts, a little Botox to his brow line and regular appointments with his stylist to ensure that the hair on his head and in his goatee remained a youthful chocolate brown. He was fond of designer clothes, preferred silk to cotton and didn't own anything made from denim or, God forbid, a synthetic fiber. He regularly wore large diamond studs in both of his ears and carried a European handbag to accommodate his BlackBerry and assorted other electronic gadgets.

In other words, Zeke was the walking definition of the metrosexual man while Angelo was the walking definition of masculinity.

Atlanta couldn't see Angelo carrying a purse, regardless of the label one gave it, and she knew he didn't dye his hair because she'd spotted a few strands of gray around his temples. As for Botox, if he indulged in it, he wasn't getting his money's worth, but he was all the more ruggedly handsome for the lines that fanned out from his eyes, which most likely were the result of squinting into the sun to catch a fly ball.

For the past decade, Zeke had dominated Atlanta's life. Under his rigid tutelage, she'd been transformed from a mousy-haired, small-town girl with big dreams and some talent into a blonde, box-office bombshell. On screen, she melted hearts and left men salivating. More than once in real life, Zeke had accused her of being frigid. Given her past, she'd thought herself incapable of the kind of intense passion she portrayed on screen. But when Atlanta was around Angelo, she was never more aware of her sexuality or of her purely feminine response to him.

It scared her.

Angelo was ticked off. His lunch with Isabella had gone well, but when he returned to his villa he found a delivery from Luca. Tucked in the basket of fresh fruit was a note. It was written in Italian, so the only word he recognized was Papa.

He crumpled it up and shoved it into his pocket before grabbing the keys to the rental car.

Damn the man. Damn him.

He had no idea where he was going, only that he

needed to get out, get away. The problem with Monta Correnti, though, was it wasn't big enough to put much distance between Angelo and his troubles. After more than an hour of driving, mostly in circles, he wound up at the one place he knew he wasn't welcome. Oddly, that made it perfect.

Lost in thought, the unexpected knock at the villa door gave Atlanta a start. It was late in the afternoon and she wasn't expecting anyone. Probably Franca, she thought, smoothing the hair back from her face. The woman was super efficient and determined that Atlanta would enjoy her stay. But it wasn't her landlady who stood on the other side of the door. It was Angelo.

Atlanta's mouth fell open before she managed to sputter out a greeting. "I wasn't expecting…company."

Angelo's in particular, though she'd thought of him incessantly all afternoon. For a moment she wondered if she'd conjured him up. But no, he was flesh and blood and all brooding male.

"Sorry to drop by unannounced," he began. "I wasn't exactly planning to come here. I just was driving around and…" His words trailed away on a frown.

It was the frown that stopped her from inviting him inside. He looked none too happy to be there and, as such, she doubted he planned to stay. So she folded her hands and waited patiently for him to say whatever it was that had compelled him to her villa.

"Can you read Italian?"

The question came out of left field. "Can I read…?"

"Italian," he said impatiently.

"A little."

"Good. Decipher this for me, okay?" He pulled a

wadded-up piece of paper from his pocket and dropped it into her palm.

Atlanta smoothed out the worst of the wrinkles. Though her grasp of the language was rudimentary at best, she understood enough that she glanced up sharply.

"It's from your father."

"I know. Even I could figure that out." He closed his eyes for a moment. "Sorry."

"It's okay." She tapped the paper with one finger. "This is personal. Are you sure you want me to read it?"

His laughter was bitter, but not directed at her. "Personal," he drawled. "Isn't that rich. The first I've heard from him in practically forever and the guy writes it in a language I can't understand." Despite the firm set of his jaw, she saw bewilderment and pain in his expression. "Read it."

My Dearest Son,
Thank you for coming to Monta Correnti. I wanted to give you a little time to get settled before coming by, but I am eager to see you.

You have grown into a fine man from everything I have read and from what your brother told me. You cannot know how glad that makes my heart.

My hope is that, like Alessandro, you will come to forgive me and we can start fresh.

With love, Papa

"He sent me a damned fruit basket," Angelo muttered as he pocketed the note Atlanta returned to him. "Can you believe that?"

"What should he send?"

"Nothing. I don't want anything from him."

But it was so plain to her he did that her heart ached. She knew what it was like to want to be loved. Angelo was no big-egoed jock now. Perhaps that was what prompted her to ask, "Do you want to come in?"

He surprised her again by saying, "I do, but first I feel like I owe you an apology for today, even if I don't think I said anything out of line."

"You didn't. I overreacted."

He shoved a hand through his hair as he exhaled, giving her the impression he'd expected her to argue. "So...we're okay?"

Not exactly. There remained an unsettling amount of attraction that she didn't know what to do with. But Atlanta nodded and smiled. As an afterthought, she added, "Well, except for the cannoli. I didn't get to finish one, let alone two."

"I guess I do owe you an apology after all." He smiled as he stepped into the foyer, and she nearly regretted her impulse to invite him inside. "What can I do to make it up to you?"

"Buy me dinner." The words were out in a rush. Being out in public with him seemed the safer bet.

"I can do that."

"I can be ready in an hour if you want to come back."

"What's wrong with right now?"

"Right now? I'm not dressed for dinner." She was wearing the same jeans and sweater set she'd had on earlier. It was fine for kicking around the village or hanging out alone at the villa, but dinner? She always dressed for dinner. Zeke said...She notched up her chin. "I'm wearing what I have on."

"Fine by me. I wasn't expecting you to change."

Simple words, a simple statement. Yet her heart did a funny little flip. For good measure she added, "And I get to pick the place."

CHAPTER SIX

ANGELO felt nervous as he ushered Atlanta to the car. He didn't like it. When it came to women, he didn't get nervous. It was the same with baseball. He was a natural. So why did he feel so out of sorts right now?

It wasn't Atlanta's fame that had his palms sweating. He'd been with well-known women before, including a couple of supermodels and a wealthy socialite who was a fixture on Page Six of the *New York Post*.

Some guys, he supposed, would confuse the woman with the breathy characters she portrayed on the big screen. Before he'd had an actual conversation with her, Angelo might have, too. But it hadn't taken long to determine that, while Atlanta shared their vulnerability and some of their spunk, she wasn't some celluloid creation concocted to appeal to the masses. Especially the male masses. She was flesh and blood. Real. Her current set of troubles would not be neatly resolved during the span of a full-length feature film. And, if his guess was right, she had a past to contend with, too, some ugly secrets that refused to stay under the rug no matter how many times she swept them there.

The two of them had that in common.

He thought about the note from his father. Atlanta was privy to far more of his past than any other woman in his life had ever been. Maybe that was why he felt nervous. Hell, maybe that was part of her overall draw. It was rare to find someone with as much baggage as he had. It was rare to have someone call him on his. In fact, he couldn't think of a single woman who ever had. They'd accepted him as the fun-loving playboy he portrayed. Atlanta had spotted the troubled man behind the façade. It was that man she spoke to.

When they reached his car, he waited until they were both settled and the engine was humming before asking, "Where to?"

"I…I don't know."

"We'll drive around the village. When you see something you like, tell me to stop."

She turned to face him. "You don't mind?"

"What's to mind?"

"A lot of men—" Zeke was implied "—like to decide the destination or at the very least know what it will be before shifting the car into drive."

"Then a lot of men don't know what they're missing," he said casually before stepping on the accelerator.

They wound up on the far side of the village at a small eatery that was really more roadside diner than restaurant. It had a small dining room, but they sat outside, enjoying the view of the neighboring shops as evening settled in.

"You're sure this is okay?" she asked not for the first time even before their beverages arrived.

"Why wouldn't it be? I'm hungry. They serve food."

"It has nothing to do with what I mentioned earlier? You know, about Zeke."

"And his tendency to call all of the shots?"

She nodded.

"Maybe a little," he agreed.

Her lips pursed. "So, you're humoring me."

"I don't see it that way." Control was important to her right now. She needed to have it. She needed to exercise it. Besides, he was curious to find out what she would do with it. And if it helped him take his mind off his father, all the better. "As I said, I have no reason to object."

Mollified, she nodded. "Okay."

"For the record, when I find a reason to draw a line in the sand, I do and I'm not likely to cross it afterward."

"Stubborn?"

"So I've been told." Most recently by Alex.

"But you're not completely intractable."

"What makes you say that?"

"You're in Italy to meet your father," she reminded him.

"Only because my brother asked me to."

"Is that the only reason?"

He said nothing.

The waiter dropped off their drinks, sparkling water for both of them. When they were alone again, she said, "I briefly considered picking your family restaurant for dinner this evening."

He sipped his water. "Why didn't you?"

"Given your reaction to your father's note, I didn't want to push you into doing something you might not be ready for," she admitted.

Her concern touched him, though a part of him was eager to shake it off. "I wouldn't have cared. He's nothing to me."

"Angelo—"

"Less than nothing." The strident words scraped his throat, making him wonder who he was trying to convince.

"It's okay to be angry," she said quietly.

"Gee, thanks for your permission."

"You know what I mean."

"Yes. I do. Sorry." He exhaled sharply.

"So, when do you plan to see your father?"

He thought about the party Isabella had told him about. He tried *not* to think about the invitation his sister had told him he was welcome to extend to a guest. He mentioned neither to Atlanta. Rather, he said casually, "I'm in no rush. I've still got a couple of weeks to kill."

"What about the restaurant? Have you seen it?"

"I ate lunch there today after you and I...parted company," he finished diplomatically.

"By yourself?"

"With Isabella. I owed her an apology."

"Isabella, hmm? You work fast. I wouldn't have guessed you'd have had an opportunity to offend any of the local women already."

"Isabella is my sister."

He liked the way the announcement caused heat to suffuse her face.

"Sister," she repeated on a slow nod.

"Half, I guess is the more accurate description. Luca remarried after Alex and I were out of the picture. He had a second family." Bitterness welled. "He decided to keep this one around."

"And you didn't know about them," she guessed.

"Not until recently." He sipped more of his water. "Nor did they apparently know about Alex and me. It came as a bit of a surprise to us all, you might say."

"I'm sorry."

He shook his head and his tone was rueful when he said, "That was my line today. As you've noticed, I'm not handling this situation very well, which is why I owed Isabella an apology. All she did was to hold out an olive branch." He shifted in his seat. "My beef isn't with her. It's with Luca."

"Yet you're in no hurry to see him, confront him."

Her simple statement cut right to the heart of it. He didn't like what that said about him. Thankfully, she changed the subject a moment later.

"Oh, my God! I nearly forgot. Something's come up. Something…embarrassing."

That got his attention. "Embarrassing for me?"

"For both of us, I'm afraid. It seems that the paparazzi you saved me from at the airport the other day got their money shot. My arrival in Rome made headlines in a couple of the rags back home."

"Sorry, Atlanta. I'd hoped to shield you from that. I take it since I was in some of those shots I was mentioned."

"Yes and some, um, assumptions were made regarding our relationship."

"They assumed we're getting away together for some R&R—Romance and Recreation," he guessed.

"According to one of the stories, I've seduced you."

"Really." His eyebrows rose along with the corners of his mouth. "You seduced me, hmm? There's a thought that's going to keep me awake into the wee hours of the morning."

"This is serious, Angelo."

He sobered a bit. "From your perspective, I know that it is. For that reason alone, if I could get my hands on those photographers, they'd be sorry they ever bought their first camera."

Atlanta was no fan of violence, but his words warmed her. When was the last time, outside of a movie set, that a man had defended her honor, let alone offered to beat up someone for her? Back to the matter at hand, she chided herself when she realized she was staring at him, a sappy smile threatening to break out.

"Aren't you the least bit upset? You're being likened to a boy toy, and Zeke is claiming that you're merely another one of my many conquests."

"When you put it like that, okay, I'm a little upset. I'm no boy, Atlanta." No, indeed, he was all man. "As for the conquest remark, well, that rubs the wrong way, too." He scratched his chin thoughtfully. "But there's an upside to this for me."

"There is?"

He smiled again. "Unlike the other recent tabloids reports about me, at least this time no one is questioning my physical ability."

She laughed because she didn't have an off-the-cuff remark handy. Not to mention that the mental image of Angelo "performing" to his physical best left her a little tongue-tied.

The sandwiches they ordered came on thickly sliced ciabatta. The cold cuts and cheese were tasty, the bread good, but none of it could hold a candle to the stuff Angelo had sampled at Rosa earlier in the day, a fact that made him feel strangely proud and definitely uneasy.

The thing that helped banish both was watching Atlanta eat. She pulled off one of the two slices of provolone and half of the salami, setting them aside with the top slice of bread. No doubt she was tallying up carb and protein grams as she went. Afterward, she went after what remained of the sandwich with dainty nibbles that barely put a dent in the hefty ciabatta. It was the damned cannoli all over again. Angelo stifled the urge to comment. Instead he went after his own sandwich with a gusto that far inflated his actual enjoyment of it.

When he glanced up, Atlanta was watching him. He took another bite and added a few sound effects as he chewed. "Mmm-mmm."

Her gaze narrowed and she set her open-faced sandwich on her plate where she piled the rest of the ingredients back on, including the second slice of ciabatta. She lifted the finished product with a flourish, her expression as steely and no-nonsense as a gunslinger's. Then she brought the sandwich to her mouth. No dainty nip for her this time. She opened wide and came away with enough to keep her chewing for the next couple minutes. He watched her the entire time, that same odd mixture of pride and unease making his skin prickle.

She wasn't able to finish the sandwich. No surprise there since the portion had been generous. Still, she'd eaten more than half of it before calling it quits and even then had gone back to loot some of the good stuff from inside.

"I really enjoyed that," she admitted, settling back in her chair on a sigh that, to Angelo's way of thinking, seemed way too close to those issued during post-coital bliss.

"I enjoyed watching you."

"So how does it rate?"

Lost as he was in carnal thoughts, the question had his mouth dropping open. "Rate?" he repeated inanely.

"You know, compared to Rosa."

"Oh. Right. Food. And Rosa." The words marched out his mouth in staccato procession.

Atlanta laughed, enjoying him as much as she'd just

enjoyed her sandwich. "I'm not even going to ask what you thought I wanted you to rate."

"Wise move, though I'll be happy to tell you."

He was back to flirting. She decided to play along. "Fine. Tell."

His brows rose. Clearly, he hadn't expected her to call him on it. Would he back down?

The answer was clear as soon as he said, "We danced about it earlier today."

"Ah, attraction."

"Let's call it what it really is. Sex."

At the coffee shop she'd gotten all riled for reasons that had nothing to do with the man sitting before her. Did he think she would again? Was he testing her?

"So we were," she said nonchalantly.

He smiled, as if pleased by the way she was rallying. Then he asked point-blank, "How long has it been for you?"

"How long has…?" She sputtered out a mild oath before regaining her composure. She was offended, she reminded herself, even as heat curled through her. "Some questions are too rude to warrant an answer. Or are you one of those men who love to kiss and tell?"

Her reprimand left him undeterred. "I'm discreet. I see no reason to brag." Then he got back to her sex life. "I'm guessing it's been a while."

She was not going to have this conversation. But she heard herself ask, "What makes you so sure?"

"Even though you ended things with Zeke about six months ago, if things weren't going well, the two of you probably weren't sleeping together for a while before then. So, it's been months, perhaps more than a year."

"What about all of the lovers I've supposedly had?"

"I'm not buying it."

She swallowed, pathetically pleased and grateful. She was back to irritated when he said, "I'm not Zeke."

"I wasn't mistaking you for him."

His eyes narrowed. "But I'm betting you've done some comparing."

She flushed guiltily and was grateful they were seated outside under the uneven glow of hanging lanterns.

"For the record," he was saying, "I'm younger, fitter and a whole lot more accommodating."

"Thanks for the heads up."

He wasn't put off by her bored attitude. He leaned over the table, lowered his voice. "I like you. I'm attracted to you. I can't promise you that whatever happens between us will last beyond Italy. I never make any kind of promises. And you may be okay with that since you aren't looking for strings. But, given our individual circumstances, a few fireworks might be a welcome diversion for both of us."

Angelo was turning her inside out with his words, but she felt no shame, nor was she visited by any bitter memories. Even her current troubles blended into the background, until the only thing left was temptation and something akin to yearning. She recalled Sara's suggestion of a vacation fling. A post-Zeke fling.

"And you can guarantee those?" she asked as sparks showered her skin.

"With a little encouragement and participation, of course." He reached over to stroke the side of her face. "Lovemaking is all about give and take. It's not just about having control, but giving it to the other person. Both parties end up satisfied that way."

His words had heat suffusing her face as well as regions of a body that had been languishing in permafrost for far longer than he assumed. Give *and* take. In her experience only one of those two verbs had ever come into play, unless she was in front of a camera with a director calling the shots.

Her voice wasn't quite steady when she asked, "Are you finished with your analysis, Dr. Freud?"

"For now. The rest can wait for another time."

Because she found herself surprisingly eager for future tutelage, Atlanta decided to change the subject. "As fascinating as I find our conversation, I'm afraid jet lag is catching up with me."

"Does that mean you want me to take you home?"

She nodded. Then, tipping her head to one side, she asked, "Mad?"

"Disappointed, but it's just as well. I don't think either of us is ready for what our raging hormones have in store."

Not ready in the least, she knew. But that didn't stop her from dreaming about it when, later that evening, she fell asleep in her bed all alone.

From his prone position on the mattress, Angelo stared up at the bedroom ceiling. As his gaze idly traced the shadows thrown from the bedside lamp, he recounted the evening.

That wasn't something he did normally, even when the evening in question ended on a far more satisfactory note. Yet he didn't feel frustrated exactly, sexually or otherwise. Like a damned moth, he just felt drawn and more curious than ever about the woman most of the world thought they knew.

He flipped to his side, recalling the way Atlanta had looked when he'd left her on her doorstep. He'd waited, and, yes, he'd hoped that she would invite him inside. Whether for a nightcap or something more, he hadn't cared. He'd only known that he hadn't wanted the evening to end. But she hadn't invited him in. Instead, she'd smiled and bade him goodnight.

With a handshake!

Left with little choice, he'd taken her hand, pumped it delicately and released it so quickly it might as well have been a poisonous snake. Patience, he'd reminded himself. He was pretty certain she was a woman who'd had some bad breaks when it came to physical intimacy. Just when he'd convinced himself of that and had turned toward his car, she'd grabbed his arm and spun him back around.

The kiss that had followed hadn't been chaste. It had been downright greedy. He'd felt teeth nip at his lower lip and fingernails bite into the flesh of his arms. It hadn't ended slowly or on a sigh. No, she'd broken it off cleanly, her breathing labored afterward.

He'd considered a pithy comeback. Hell, he'd considered hauling her back into his arms and having a second go at it. Only her expression had stopped him. It had been neither smug nor frightened. Rather, she'd looked uncertain, confused.

For him, sex had never been complicated, partly because he was smart enough to know women often viewed the act differently. They tried to inject emotions into the mix, which could cause problems if a guy let things progress too far. Mindful of his parents and the disaster they had made of not only their marriage but of their children's lives, he'd been careful not to let that happen.

So, why was he feeling every bit as confused and uncertain as Atlanta had looked? He turned out the lamp and gave his pillow a couple of punches. It was going to be a long night.

* * *

Angelo had no firm plans for the following day, which was just as well. He woke in pain not long after the sun rose.

"Damned shoulder," he muttered, although it wasn't his only source of discomfort. "Damned woman."

He swung his legs over the side of the mattress and scraped the hand of his good arm over his jaw, eyeing the pills on the nightstand as he did so. In the end, he decided to do what he had for the past year of his career: play through the pain.

By mid-afternoon, with nothing more to occupy his time than Italian television programs and a couple of old *Sports Illustrated* magazines he'd brought with him, he was surly and sick of his own company, so he got in the car and headed out for a drive. He didn't plan his destination, at least not consciously, but he wound up at Atlanta's villa. This time, however, when he knocked at the door it was a dark-haired woman who answered. Given the wicker basket of linens on the floor at her feet, he figured she was there to do the cleaning.

"Hi... I mean, *ciao*. I was looking for Atlanta Jackson. I take it she's not here."

"No." But the woman's expression brightened. Her tone held a little awe when she said, "You are Angelo Casali."

Finally, someone recognized him. He grinned in return. "Yes, I am."

"It is such a pleasure to meet you."

"Thanks."

Her obvious excitement. The wide-eyed adoration. He lapped both up. He was just about to ask her if she wanted his autograph when she added, "I know your family well. I attended school with Isabella. I had a crush on Valentino."

Angelo's smile faltered. She knew his family, but apparently she'd never heard of his multimillion-dollar baseball career, which was fading as fast as the season. How ironic that the New York Angel's only claim to fame here was as Luca Casali's son.

The young woman was saying, "I met Alessandro while he was in Monta Correnti. He was at Rosa one evening when my husband and I dined there." She tipped her head to one side and studied Angelo. "You both have the look of your father. You have his eyes."

Angelo backed up a step. He cared for neither the comparison she was making nor the connection it defined. "I have to be going."

"Do you wish to leave a message for Miss Jackson?"

"No. I'll…" He shook his head and said a second time, "No."

The woman was still standing in the open doorway staring after him when he climbed into the car. He revved its engine to life, shifted into gear and hit the gas. The tires spat gravel and gave a little squeal as he sped away. He didn't care. He had to get out of there. Just as Atlanta had the day before at the coffee shop, Angelo found himself running from the past.

It was the present that caused him to slow down before he hit the first bend in the road, which was a good thing considering the sharp turns up ahead. Another fifty feet and the road became as curvy as the woman walking along the side of it.

Atlanta.

She was more strolling than walking, given the leisurely pace of her long-legged stride. She looked more relaxed than he'd ever seen her. Fresh air and the Italian countryside agreed with her. She held a bouquet

of wildflowers in one hand. Her signature blonde hair
was partly obscured beneath a cap that, upon closer
inspection, he realized was emblazoned with the logo
of a rival ball club. Even so, the sight of her made him
smile. Some of his tension ebbed away, only to be replaced with a different sort of restlessness when she
spotted him and waved. He pulled the car over and got
out, leaning against the hood while he waited for her to
reach him.

When she did he asked, "Getting in a little exercise?"

"That wasn't my primary objective, but yes."

He was glad to hear she didn't feel the need to walk
off last night's carbohydrate indulgence. The woman
who just the day before had been racked with guilt over
a couple of cannoli was making progress.

"Are you heading back?" he asked.

She glanced at her wristwatch. "Not quite yet. My
landlady, Franca, is there. She insists on changing the
sheets every day, though I've told her I'm not that picky.
I left because I didn't want to be underfoot."

"Interested in some company?"

She fussed with the ponytail that spilled out the back
of the hat. "I wouldn't mind it."

Initially, Atlanta had gone for a walk to clear her head.
The day was perfect for it, so sunny and warm. But how
was a woman supposed to keep her head clear when
the man responsible for clouding it up was now asking
to join her?

She could tell him no. She'd turned Angelo down
more than once, and for things more consequential than
a stroll down a country road. Despite the bruises he
claimed his ego had endured, it hadn't stopped him from

coming back or from being a friend, even if it was clear he had more than friendship on his mind.

Still, the friendship was an unexpected gift. She'd never had a male friend before. For that matter, with the exception of Sara, Atlanta had precious few female ones. Hollywood wasn't the sort of town where one could cultivate deep bonds of any sort easily. Too many people had an agenda or an angle to work. Very little was ever as it seemed on the surface, a fact Atlanta knew all too well.

"I want to thank you," she said.

His brows shot up. "For what?"

"For being a friend."

He stuffed his hands in the front pockets of his jeans. "That's just what a guy wants to hear."

"Sorry, it's just that I don't have many friends and I really need one right now."

"I know." His tone was serious when he said, "Same goes for me."

"Oh." She smiled, pleased.

"Just to be clear, though. I still want to sleep with you."

She stopped walking and faced him. "Why do you do that?"

"Do what?"

"Hide behind macho come-on lines."

She expected him to deny it. Instead, he replied, "For the same reason that you fall back on your plastic Hollywood smile."

She sobered.

"Yeah." He nodded. "I can tell the difference between a real Atlanta Jackson smile and the ones you manufacture for the masses."

"Touché." She plucked at the petals of one of the flowers in her bouquet.

"How about we make a deal?"

"I'm listening."

"How about if we're real with one another?"

"Flaws and all?" she wanted to know.

"Why not? What's to lose? The way I see it, everyone thinks they've got us figured out based on all of the media hype. We both know they're wrong."

"So, you're not an arrogant athlete with more testosterone than intelligence?"

"No more than you are a self-absorbed starlet who uses and discards men by the dozen." At her startled expression, he said, "That was the quote I read on an Internet site the other day."

Her eyelids flickered. "God, we're a pair."

"Only if you believe the tabloids," he said. "So, deal?"

"Deal."

They started walking again. A few minutes later, Angelo bent to pick a flower similar to the ones in her bouquet. He handed it to her.

"Thanks."

"They're pretty."

"I thought so. I'm going to look them up online later, find out what they are."

"Is that how you're filling your time these days, trolling the Internet?"

"Yes, and, before you say anything, I'm loving it. I haven't had a real vacation, and by real I mean a do-nothing sort of vacation, in years. In fact, I don't think I've ever had one," she said wryly.

All of her downtime away from a movie set was spent promoting a project, a product or herself. That was

Zeke's idea. Two birds with one stone and all that. Even the supposedly romantic getaways the pair of them had taken over the years had included jaunts to public places where the paparazzi were sure to spot them. Indeed, Atlanta sometimes wondered if Zeke wasn't responsible for some of the anonymous tips to the tabloids that had divulged their locations and left her ducking for cover.

"Neither have I, and for good reason," Angelo was saying. "Two days with little to do and I'm going stir crazy."

"How can you be bored here?" She spread her arms wide.

"I'm not bored, I just feel…trapped."

She turned, not sure she'd heard him correctly. His frown told her that she had.

"I know about feeling trapped," she said quietly.

He was still frowning, but something in his expression had changed, softened in a way she couldn't quite define. "I think you do."

"Anything I can do to help?"

"A friend to a friend?"

"That's right."

Though the way he was looking at her suggested more than friendly feelings.

"Then, yes." His gaze grew intense as he studied her. Would he bare his soul and divulge some of his secrets? Would he kiss her? He did neither. Instead, he snatched the ball cap off her head. "You can set a match to this. God! The team manages to win one stinking World Series and suddenly everyone becomes a fan."

She knew it was his intent to lighten the situation, so she allowed her laughter to ring out in the late afternoon. Another time, perhaps she wouldn't let him off the hook so easily.

"Which team should I root for?"

"The best one out there."

"Yours?"

"The Rogues." Afterward, his expression darkened again, leaving her to wonder if it was mere clarification he sought with his answer or outright distance.

CHAPTER SEVEN

ATLANTA lost track of the time as they walked, but the lengthening shadows of the trees, as well as the indelicate protests of her empty stomach, told her it was getting close to dinner. Regardless, Franca would be done changing the linens by now.

They headed back to her villa, stopping when they reached his car. Though he probably found the gesture foolish, she handed him the flowers that she'd collected. They were drooping a little now.

"If you put them in water they should perk back up," she said, not at all confident that would be the case.

"Thanks."

He looked as ridiculous holding them as she would have looked outfitted in a catcher's pads squatting behind home plate. He'd probably toss them out the window before he hit the first curve. Men weren't sentimental.

Angelo surprised her by snapping the stem on one bloom. After tugging off her hat for the second time that day, he tucked the flower behind her ear.

"My Italian can use a lot of work, as you well know, but I'm aware of one word that applies in this case. *Bella.*"

Beautiful. She'd been called that before, in several different languages both on-screen and off. This time the compliment curled around her and she luxuriated in its embrace.

"Thank you."

The breeze kicked up. Without the ball cap he found so offensive, it sent ribbons of her hair across her face. The yellow blossom tumbled free from its perch at her ear. He caught it before it could hit the ground.

"It doesn't want to stay put," she murmured as her heart kicked out an extra beat. He was standing so close she could feel the heat emanating from his body.

"I guess I cut the stem a little too short."

"You could try another one."

"Yeah? You mean keep at it till I get it right?"

Atlanta swallowed, nodded.

"You know, you have a point," he said slowly, seriously. "Not everything works the way we want it to the first time." He leaned back against the car and rested his hands lightly on her waist. "Like last night."

"What about last night?"

"That kiss you gave me."

"You had a problem with it?" she asked, trying to sound insulted rather than insecure.

"I wouldn't call it a problem. It's just that if I'd been in control I would have done things a little differently."

Angelo's choice of words was deliberate, she knew. He was making a not so subtle reference to Zeke, as well as offering a not so subtle reminder that last night he'd let her call the shots, everything from where to eat to how to end the evening.

"You were a perfect gentleman, by the way, a fact I appreciated."

His gaze sharpened slightly. "Were you worried that I wouldn't be?"

"If I had been I wouldn't have agreed to have dinner with you," she replied seriously.

He nodded. "And what about tonight?"

Because she found the invitation to spend another evening with him way too tempting, she dodged it by asking, "When are you going to get around to visiting with the relatives you came to Italy to see?"

"When I can no longer avoid it," he said pointedly. "So, about tonight?"

"All right, under one condition."

His eyes narrowed. "What might that be?"

"You have to tell me something about yourself. Something no one else knows. I figure that's only fair since so much of my dirty laundry is out in the air."

He nodded slowly. "Okay, but I have a condition of my own. I get to pick the place tonight."

"Deal," Atlanta said, sure she'd gotten the better end of the bargain.

Back at the villa, she hurriedly changed her clothes. Angelo insisted she needn't bother, with the exception of the ball cap. But that meant she had to do something different with her hair and, while she was at it, it seemed a shame not to slip into one of the pretty skirts and new blouses she'd brought with her. So while he paced around the courtyard, she was in her room, primping for another evening out.

She wasn't sure what had happened to her resolve to steer clear of men in general and Angelo Casali in particular. Nor could she say why she'd told him things about her relationship with Zeke that she'd only admitted to a few people, and then with mixed reactions.

"Don't bite the hand that feeds you," her agent had warned when Atlanta had confided her unhappiness a year earlier. "You might be a box-office draw, but Zeke wields a scary amount of power in this town. So what if he likes to tell you how to wear your hair or which entree to order at Spago? Nine times out of ten, he's right. The guy has the Midas touch when it comes to building careers. A million other wannabes would be only too happy to heed his advice."

Angelo, however, had understood that it wasn't advice Zeke imparted, but rules. He'd created her, named her, handcrafted every aspect of her past and present. He'd controlled her, every bit as much as her stepfather had, caging her in and making her feel trapped, helpless.

But just as she'd broken free from her stepfather's grip, she'd wrested herself from Zeke's control. No man was going to bully her or boss her around. That included Angelo, even if she'd opted to let him pick the location for tonight's meal.

She felt confident and unconcerned when, once they were seated in his car, she asked, "So, where are we heading for dinner?"

He tapped his fingers on the steering wheel. "My villa."

"Your villa?" Her nerves kicked into high gear right along with the sports coupe.

"We can go somewhere else if you'd rather," he said.

His offer quelled her concern. Now Atlanta was intrigued, "Why your villa?"

"My sister made this incredible feast for me the other night. I have a lot of leftovers. More than I can eat in this lifetime. I thought we could dine *alfresco*. The view from my patio is five-star.

"Is that the only reason?" When he shook his head, she added, "I didn't think so."

She waited for him to make some flirty comment about wanting to be alone with her. He didn't. Rather, he sighed. "Monta Correnti is small. Everyone here knows my father or someone in my family."

"You should be used to being recognized," she reminded him. "It's not like you're anonymous when you go out in New York or anywhere in America, for that matter."

"That's just it. I'm not recognized here, Atlanta. No one here knows Angelo Casali." He was talking about the ballplayer. "Here I am only Luca's long-lost son."

"Angelo." Understanding the source of his pain, she reached out to him. Then she screamed, "Look out!"

Angelo had been watching her rather than the road, a dangerous proposition, especially on this winding stretch. As a result, he wasn't quite ready for the hairpin turn ahead. To avoid collision with a tree, he stepped on the brake and yanked the steering wheel to one side. The car skidded on gravel for what seemed like a lifetime before the tire found traction.

He grunted and bit back the worst of an oath as pain shot from his shoulder. As he cupped it with his hand he asked, "Are you okay?"

"Fine," Atlanta said. "But I don't think you are."

He tried to lie around a grimace. "I'm good."

She wasn't buying it. "Your shoulder is bothering you again."

"More like still," he admitted.

"Are you taking something for the pain?"

"When it becomes unbearable."

"From what I've observed that must be most of the time."

Angelo didn't deny it. Instead, he said, "The pills the

doctor prescribed make me tired and a little foggy. I've played through pain before."

"We're not talking about a baseball game, Angelo. This is your health, your quality of life. You can't keep on this way. Eventually, I'm guessing your shoulder is going to require surgery."

Surgery. The S word. After which would come the R word. Not rehabilitation, but retirement.

"Look, I'm fine," he said a second time. He didn't need to see her blink to know his tone carried an edge. "Sorry."

"No. I'm sorry. It's not my business."

It wasn't. Yet he heard himself say, "I'm scared, Atlanta."

Her gaze snapped to his. "Of having surgery?"

That was only a small part of his fear. He was far more unnerved that he might lose his overall identity. But he nodded. As he maneuvered the car back onto the road, he said, "Well, there it is. The secret no one else knows. I'm a big baby when it comes to the thought of going under the knife."

Her smile was the plastic Hollywood variety. She knew he was a liar.

The sun was just starting to set when they reached Angelo's villa. Atlanta was out of the car before he could come around to open her door.

"I didn't think it was possible to top the view from my place, but this does. And you have a pool. Very nice."

"I also have a hot tub."

"I'm going to have a talk with my travel agent when I get back."

"No need to be jealous. I'm willing to share. We can take a dip in it later if you'd like."

She pursed her lips in mock dismay. "Darn. I don't have a suit."

Blue eyes twinkled. "I don't mind."

She deflected his flirting by saying, "I bet the hot tub feels like heaven on your shoulder."

He scowled and started to walk away before turning back. Snagging her wrist, he hauled her close. "Let's get something straight. I may be on the injured list, but I'm not out of the game."

She wasn't put off in the least by his temper. "Are you talking figuratively or literally?"

"Both," he said, before bringing his mouth down on hers.

Atlanta expected his kiss to be hard, punishing even. Angelo was angry. He was scared, too. Not of having shoulder surgery, though that was his claim. It went beyond that, she was sure. Which was why she allowed the kiss, hoping, foolishly perhaps, that he would find some comfort in it.

It was clear he hadn't when he broke off abruptly and stepped away from her. Shoving a hand through his hair, he said, "If you want to leave now, I'll understand."

She frowned. "Why would I want to leave?"

"I shouldn't have done that. I…I know you have some issues regarding…control. And with, um, no meaning no."

Her throat ached as his words pierced the barrier protecting her heart. "I didn't say no."

"If you had, I wouldn't have kissed you," he said earnestly.

She nodded. "If I had, I wouldn't have let you."

"So, you want to stay?"

"I was promised a meal."

Angelo ushered her inside the villa. The main living

space was larger than the one in hers and, she decided from the well-appointed furnishings, professionally decorated.

"This is very nice." The quality of the pieces was obvious. The owner had expensive taste and the bank account to indulge it.

Angelo's tone was wry. "You might want to reserve your opinion until you've seen the kitchen."

She understood what he meant a moment later. Rustic was the word that came to mind. The stove was a big black behemoth.

"Oh, my God."

"Exactly, although Isabella managed to create a feast in here." His expression brightened. "Hey, didn't you play a chef in one of your movies?"

"Sous chef, but the operative word here is played. This is beyond my talents as either an actress or an amateur cook." She exhaled softly as she turned in a semi-circle. "I don't suppose there's a microwave stashed in one of the cupboards?"

"Nope. And, believe me, I've checked every last one of them. Apparently the guy who owns this place stopped short of renovating the kitchen. This is original to the house."

"So I can see. What's wrong with the owner? He's not a fan of eating?"

"He's not a fan of cooking. My sister said he doesn't spend much time in Monta Correnti and when he does, he takes his meals elsewhere." Angelo's brows drew together. "You know, I have a feeling that's what my brother had in mind for me when he booked my accommodations."

She chuckled. "Sounds like a bit of a set-up."

"I'll find a way to make him pay," he muttered as he crossed to the equally ancient-looking refrigerator.

While Angelo pulled out an assortment of covered bowls, Atlanta rooted through cabinets and drawers, and came up with plates and silverware. They decided to eat the pasta cold, pairing it with fat slices of thick-crusted Italian bread. She decided to indulge in what Zeke had considered an absolute no-no and combined olive oil and some dried herbs she found in the pantry in a shallow bowl to dip the bread in. Then she took the dishes, utensils, bread and herbed oil out to the patio table. Night had fallen. Hanging lanterns illuminated the pool and patio area, while down the hillside the lights from scattered homes mirrored the stars that winked in the sky. Angelo joined her a moment later with the pasta, a bottle of wine and two glasses whose thin stems were wedged between his fingers.

"No wine for me, thanks," she said.

Even so, he set one down in front of her plate. "Just in case you change your mind. Nothing brings out the rich flavors of a meal like a nice glass of wine."

"Okay, half a glass."

Before they finished their meal, Atlanta had consumed a second half. Angelo was right about the wine. It complemented the flavor of the tomato sauce perfectly. Indeed, she couldn't recall the last time she'd enjoyed a meal as much as this one.

"This is incredible," she said, forking up the last bite of pasta. "I've always been a fan of Italian cuisine, although I can't quite place all of the flavors in this sauce."

"It contains a special kind of basil. It's grown locally. Very exclusive." A deep groove formed between his brows. "When I arrived here the other day and smelled the sauce simmering in the kitchen, I remembered going out with Alex and my father to pick the herb. I would have been a preschooler."

"I've heard it said that smell is one of the most potent senses when it comes to memory recall."

"I believe it."

He didn't sound happy about it, so she didn't ask if the outing with his father and brother was a good memory. Even if it were, the intervening years surely would have soured it.

She'd finished off her wine. He pointed to the empty glass. "Would you like some more?"

"No, I've had enough."

"I believe the word they use here is *basta*," he told her.

"That's right." She nodded. "It's a handy word to know."

"Just be careful," he warned. "If you use it too often you're likely to miss out on a lot of…adventure."

Angelo expected Atlanta to say she wasn't up for any more adventure in her life. He wouldn't blame her for feeling that way, especially with a new scandal brewing over the photos that had been snapped of the two of them in Rome's airport. Instead, she studied him in the soft light that cascaded from the patio's scattered lanterns.

"I guess I'll have to use my best judgment, then."

"You do that."

Angelo finished his Chianti and leaned back in his chair on a contented sigh that morphed into a yelp of pain when he tried to stack his hands behind his head. He lowered his arms immediately and reached for his shoulder before he could think better of it.

Atlanta's eyes were wide with concern.

"Don't say it." His words held more of a plea than a warning.

"Fine. I won't ask about surgery or rehabilitation or quality of life," she promised. "But I am curious."

The pain was abating. He squinted at her. "About what?"

"What do you plan to do after baseball?"

After? The word hit him with the force of a fastball to the chest. There was no after. Just as he'd convinced himself over the years that there had been no before. Baseball was both his alpha and omega.

"I'm not going anywhere." Even before she raised her eyebrows, he knew he sounded belligerent. That didn't stop him from adding, "The Rogues still need me. I'll be suiting up next season, make no mistake."

"I'm not talking about next season. Or even the season after that. You can't play ball forever, Angelo."

It wasn't anything he hadn't heard from other people, including younger players speculating on what the future held for them post-career. Usually, Angelo deflected the conversation with a witty comeback. This time, seated next to Atlanta in the cool evening air, he not only accepted reality, he met it head-on.

Gazing up at the stars, he admitted, "I don't know what I'll do."

"You have lots of options."

He did. He could branch off into coaching. One of the farm teams had already approached him with an offer. He could buy one of the existing franchises when it came up for sale. Ownership certainly held appeal. Money wasn't an object. The endorsement well showed no signs of drying up, despite his latest injury. But…

"Baseball is everything."

"Not everything," Atlanta replied softly.

"To me it is. It saved me. Literally. Baseball and Alex, they were what kept me from becoming a statistic."

"What do you mean?" she asked.

This wasn't something he talked about freely, let alone with a beautiful woman who had her own set of problems. But the timing, the woman who was willing to listen, they both seemed right.

"I was bound for trouble and taking the express train to get there. I was too young and too stupid to care about consequences. And I was just plain ticked off," he could admit now.

"At your father," she guessed.

"Him, yeah. And my mom." Angelo snorted. "Hell, I was angry at everyone." The sky held a million stars. He concentrated on one of them and continued. "No one seemed to give a damn about my brother and me. Our mom came home drunk most nights. She worked in public relations as a consultant. She kept a roof over our heads and, when she remembered to go grocery shopping, food in the pantry. But, honestly, I don't know how she managed to keep a job."

"Not all alcoholics are falling-down drunks. Some are quite capable of leading dual lives, at least for a while."

"That was Cindy. She wasn't a mean person, just disinterested in motherhood and, I think, angry with Luca that their marriage hadn't worked out. From what little she said on the subject, they'd met while she was vacationing here, she got pregnant and they got married. They barely knew one another. Not exactly the recipe for long-term success."

"No."

"Anyway, I think she was desperate to stay young and free of responsibility."

"That's pretty hard to do when you have twins," Atlanta inserted.

"Yeah, well, it didn't stop her. She spent more time out partying at trendy nightclubs than she did at home with Alex and me."

Maybe, Angelo realized now, that was why he'd never cared for the fun-loving party girls who hung around outside the stadium after games hoping to hook up with the players. They were a little too reminiscent of Cindy and her irresponsible ways for his taste.

The star he was staring at winked as if urging him on.

"Some of our teachers tried to help, but they could only do so much without state intervention. Cindy was good at avoiding that. Whenever she was called in for a parent-teacher conference or visited by a social worker, she would ramp up the tears and promise to change her ways. They believed her. Hell, Alex and I believed her."

"Those kinds of promises are impossible not to believe coming from someone you need and love," Atlanta said in a voice that sounded both sad and knowing.

"Things would be good for a while, but then she'd start going out again."

The stars blurred out of focus. Angelo swallowed. His mother had abandoned her sons, too. Not physically, but emotionally.

"Didn't your father at least help out financially?"

He shook his head. "According to her, the reason Alex and I wound up in the States to begin with was that Luca was broke and couldn't provide for us. He was selling food from a roadside stand at that point." Angelo's tone turned frosty. "Eventually things turned around. He managed to open a restaurant, remarry and support a second family."

"He never contacted you and Alex?"

"Once. We were eighteen and already living in New York. He managed to track us down through some shirt-tail relative of our mother's. I was so ticked off at him that I hung up the telephone a few minutes into the conversation. Busted the receiver in two." He snorted out a laugh that held no humor.

"You had a right to be angry."

Hearing her say it opened the floodgate. During the past twenty years, he'd shared his private pain with no one except his twin. He found it surprisingly easy to tell Atlanta, "Luca forgot all about Alex and me. When you come right down to it, he abandoned us!"

His words echoed down the hillside.

"I'm sorry, Angelo." Atlanta reached across the table to lay one of her hands over his.

"It was a long time ago."

"Not so long that it doesn't still hurt."

And it did. The pain in his heart throbbed as intensely as the one in his shoulder. His throat constricted with emotions he rarely allowed to the surface. Not trusting himself to speak, he nodded.

CHAPTER EIGHT

"So, TELL me how baseball saved you," Atlanta said after a long moment. "Did you play for your high school's team?"

"No. I didn't have the grades to make the school's team. You had to pull at least a C average in all of your classes to suit up one week to the next. I was lucky to be passing. If not for a couple of teachers who believed in social promotion, I don't think Alex and I would have graduated the same year." He swallowed before saying, "I wasn't much of a studier and I have a hard time with letters. Some of them like to scramble up on me."

"You're dyslexic."

"They didn't use that term as much back then, but, yeah. I'm dyslexic."

"So, where does baseball enter this picture?" she asked.

"Not long after I hotwired a cherry-red Porsche."

"How old were you?"

"Fifteen."

"Fifteen? You can't drive at that age."

"Not legally, but I'd had a lot of practice." Some of his good humor returned and he sent a wink in her direction. "I'd had a lot of practice at other things by that age, too, sweetheart."

She shook her head on a weary laugh. "Just go on with the story, please."

"Okay. By then Cindy was dead, and Alex and I were in the foster-care system. We'd already run away from a home in Boston and had lived on the streets for a while, dodging social workers and police. You meet people there." He sobered as black-edged memories swirled in. "They make certain things sound…acceptable, even though you know they aren't."

"Things like stealing a car?"

"Yeah. They turn crime into a rite of passage for misguided kids looking for a place to belong. Alex wanted no part of it. To this day, he doesn't know how close I came to being completely sucked under," Angelo said quietly.

"How did you wind up in New York?"

"The people I was running with in Boston had friends in the Bronx. They said they could find work for me. Alex didn't like it. He went with me to New York, determined to keep me out of trouble. One night, I was supposed to deliver the stolen car to a chop shop. I got the street wrong." He shook his head. "Dyslexic, remember?"

"Then what?"

"When Alex came to see me in jail, social services swooped in. He was assigned a foster home in Brooklyn. The father was a no-nonsense former U.S. Marine. Big Mike, they called him. While I was awaiting my court date the guy pulled some strings and, after spending a few weeks in juvie, I got sent there."

This wasn't part of his official bio. Long ago, Angelo's agent had talked him out of sharing any of the truly unsavory particulars. Fans rooted for underdogs, but there was no sense in making them squeamish.

"Were you found guilty?" Atlanta asked.

He nodded. "Grand theft auto, a felony. Even though I was a juvenile I was looking at some serious time. I had already racked up a couple of other minor offenses back in Boston. This made me a repeat offender as far as the DA in New York was concerned. So he charged me as an adult. I was facing time in juvenile detention until my eighteenth birthday, after which time I would be moved to the state penitentiary to finish out the rest of my sentence. But Big Mike, he was the foster dad, he went out on a limb for me at my sentencing hearing. He told the judge not to write me off. He said I was smart and had potential to turn my life around, but tossing me in the pen with the adult population would all but ensure I became a career criminal. Mike felt what I really needed was a good attitude adjustment and to have my energy refocused."

"And the judge listened?" Atlanta asked, sounding as surprised as Angelo had been twenty-some years earlier.

"Mike's word carried a lot of weight with the court." He snorted out a laugh. "For good reason, as it turned out. The guy knew how to adjust attitudes and refocus energy. The first night I was in his home he sat me down at the kitchen table and point-blank told me that if I blew the second chance he'd just gotten me, he'd personally see to it that I wound up behind bars. That's not all he told me, but I'll spare your delicate sensibilities and won't repeat the rest of his lecture."

"You were scared straight."

"Damned right. The guy was huge and intimidating as hell. He meant business. He also cared. What really kept me on the straight and narrow, though, was baseball. Mike coached a team in a recreational league. I'd always liked baseball. I'd always been good at it despite no formal training. But when I started playing on Mike's team…" He shook his head, words failing him.

Atlanta's expression softened with understanding. "So, baseball saved your life."

He nodded. "That's why it's all I can imagine doing, even though I know I can't do it forever. Given your circumstances, you probably feel the same about acting."

A shadow passed over her face. "I love it. And you're right. Acting saved me in a way, too." It was gone by the time she went on. "But if I never starred in another movie like the ones I've been making for the past decade, I'd be okay with that."

"Liar," he taunted, sure she couldn't mean it.

But her tone was emphatic. "I'm being honest, Angelo. I'm tired of the roles I've been playing. I've wanted to move in a different direction for a while now. During the past few years I've been approached by indie film makers with screenplays that have had me salivating despite the low pay and nearly nonexistent production budgets."

"What's stopped you from doing them?"

"Zeke." She shook her head then. "No. That's too neat of an explanation and not entirely accurate. The messier truth is I've been afraid. The moviegoing public loves Atlanta Jackson, the vulnerable vixen. But would they love me in a less-than-sexy role?"

Surprised, he asked, "Is that the kind of part you want to play?"

"If it had some real meat. I've also given some thought to directing. I've learned a lot from my time in front of the camera." She lifted her hands. "The bottom line is I want to be taken seriously, Angelo."

"I take you seriously."

His reply had her flustered again. She rallied quickly. "Thank you. Unfortunately, in my business, women, especially attractive women, only seem to earn accolades when their looks are diminished."

"You want more recognition in the industry?"

"Of course I do. But ultimately I want what that represents."

"Respect."

"Exactly. That's what I want from my peers in the industry."

"You don't think you have it now?" he asked in disbelief. "I'm betting most actors would give their eye-teeth to be you or to have the chance to work with you. You're one of the hottest properties on the planet, Atlanta. Plunk you in the lead role and, no matter what the movie is about, it's destined to become a blockbuster and rake in millions if not billions of dollars worldwide."

"That's not a commentary on my talent. It only means that fans like the way I look and they've gobbled up all of the poor-little-rich-girl stories Zeke planted in the media over the years. Don't get me wrong. I'm grateful for the opportunities I've had. At one point the money was enough to keep me happy and make me feel safe."

"Safe? That's an odd word choice."

"Um, you know, secure. Financially speaking." Despite the hasty clarification, he didn't think that was really what Atlanta meant. Since he'd just bared his soul, he couldn't help but feel a little disappointed that she was still holding back. She was saying, "I've got more money than I can spend in this lifetime, assuming Zeke's palimony suit doesn't leave me in the poorhouse."

"The guy is suing you for palimony?" he asked incredulously.

She rattled off a monthly sum that left Angelo

staggered. "He claims he neglected other business opportunities in order to put my career first."

"He's also claiming you did the horizontal mambo with his son and half the men in Hollywood. We both know the guy is delusional."

"Thank you."

"For what? For paying attention? I may not have known you long, Atlanta, but it's plain to me the kind of person you are…and the kind of person you aren't."

She swallowed and shrugged. "That's neither here nor there. Getting back to my point, despite being money-makers, only a couple of my movies received positive reviews. The majority were panned."

"To hell with the critics." Angelo fumed on her behalf. He'd endured similar armchair analyses from so-called experts over the years. "What do they know?"

She sighed. "They know good acting, and so do I. I'm capable of it, too. I just haven't found the right vehicle to stretch my talent. With Zeke, it became increasingly clear over the past few years that I never would. Every time I wanted to so much as read a script from a little-known screenwriter or got wind of a project that didn't require me to show my cleavage, he vetoed it."

"Is that why you finally left him?"

"I'd had enough," she said softly.

"Good for you."

"When I first met Zeke, I thought he was my savior, but it turned out I'd merely traded one male keeper for another."

"How so?"

She blinked as if just realizing what she'd said. He doubted she knew how haunted or sad she looked. It was her expression that kept him from pushing when she said, "We'll save that for another day. Do you realize it's nearly midnight?"

He stood and came around the table, where he offered her his hand. "Tomorrow then."

"Excuse me?" she asked as she rose to her feet.

"Tomorrow is another day. We can pick up where we left off. We could do dinner again."

"Angelo—"

"You don't have to tell me any deep, dark secrets. But if you do, you can trust me not to share anything I learn with another person." He lifted her hand to his mouth, kissed the back of it. "You'll find me a good listener, Atlanta. Every bit as good as you were tonight when I bared my soul."

"Then maybe you'll take a bit of advice. You're here to see your father, Angelo. You can't keep avoiding him by spending all of your time with me."

"You're the only reason this trip is tolerable." When Atlanta opened her mouth to protest, he added, "Don't worry about Luca. My father and I will have our talk. A family gathering is planned. I'll see him then and get to meet the rest of the clan." He couldn't quite keep the dread from his tone.

"I'm sure it won't be as bad as all that."

"Maybe not." He smiled. "You and I will skip out early. I see no point in staying for more than a few introductions and some small talk."

That had Atlanta blinking. "You're asking me to come with you?"

"I could use an ally."

"It's a family party, Angelo."

"They're strangers," he corrected. "The only thing we have in common is DNA."

He thought of Isabella and guilt nipped. The description didn't seem fair. His sister was kind, interesting and spirited. He liked her, admired her. The fragile bond he already felt went beyond the Casali blue eyes and a blunt chin. Under other circumstances…

But the circumstances couldn't be changed, which meant he was left to make the best of them.

"There's no need to give me your answer right now. You can think about it. As for tomorrow, I'll call early in the day, so you can figure out what our plans will be and what I should wear."

She tipped her head to one side. "You want me to tell you what to wear?"

"No. I just want to be with you. But if that's what it takes…"

He pulled her tight against him and kissed her with more passion than was wise. Was he testing her or testing himself? She sighed her consent as their lips parted. A moment later, however, her tone was no breathy whisper when she added, "We need to get one thing straight."

"And that is?" He ran his knuckles down the sides of her ribcage before resting his hands on her waist and was pleased when he felt her tremble.

Her voice remained steady and strong when she said, "We share the decision-making. Okay?"

As he lowered his mouth to hers for the second time, he whispered, "I've got no problem with that."

Atlanta was still in bed when Angelo called the following morning.

And the morning after that.

And the morning after that.

It became their habit to spend the better part of the day together and then share the evening meal. In addition to eating in, they'd dined at nearly every place in Monta Correnti. Except for Rosa and Sorella, of course.

Afterward, they talked, kissed and bade one another goodnight. It was unexpected and sweet. What was happening between them was neither friendship nor a fling. An exact definition failed her, but she knew one thing: it was becoming an exquisite kind of torture.

On this morning, Angelo's deep voice reached through the phone like a caress.

"Did you sleep well?"

She'd barely slept at all. Again. Between Angelo's increasingly bold kisses and her barely restrained responses to those kisses, she'd passed the better part of another night tossing and turning. While her legs had become tangled in the sheets, her mind had been free to roam. Time and again it strayed to sex…with Angelo. If the skill he'd shown with his mouth was any indication, the ultimate act would be good. Very good. At least from her perspective. But how would he rate the experience? Old insecurities bubbled back.

Zeke had been critical of her lovemaking.

"It's a good thing your male fans aren't privy to how inept you are in the sack, love. Ticket sales would tank."

The memory had her stammering as she tried to speak to Angelo now.

"I…I…"

"I know. Me, too."

His voice held humor, but it wasn't directed at her. She pulled the lapels of her silk pajamas together, gathered her wits and struggled to a sitting position.

"So, what do you want to do today?"

"Do you really have to ask? I think you know what

I'd like to do today. It's the same thing I wanted to do last night and the night before and the night before."

Atlanta levered the phone away from her mouth so he wouldn't hear her staggered breathing. Angelo broke the silence with a chuckle.

"Okay, I won't go there." Laughter rumbled again before he lowered his voice. In a silken whisper he added, "Yet. The day's young. There's plenty of time to revisit my original answer later on."

"Sightseeing!" she all but shouted.

"Sightseeing?"

In a less zealous tone, she told him, "The woman who owns the villa I'm renting said some medieval fortress ruins are located not that far away. We'd have to drive some and then walk a ways since they are on a remote hilltop, but I'm up for some exercise."

"So am I," he quipped. "Or at least I can be at a moment's notice."

Despite her popping hormones, she couldn't help but smile. "I'm talking about walking, Angelo."

"There are other, more stimulating ways to increase your heart rate, you know."

"Yes. A simple conversation with you is one of them." She waited for his comeback, something cocky and off-color, but the phone line remained silent. "Angelo?"

"You shouldn't tell a guy something like that," he said at last, sounding much too serious.

"Why?"

"It might give him ideas."

"From what I can tell, you have plenty of ideas already." Feeling emboldened, she took the initiative to flirt. "What are you wearing?"

"You want to know what I'm wearing?" It was apparent in his tone that her boldness took him aback.

She laughed. "I'm wearing a cotton sheet and a smile. So, what about you?"

"Apparently one article of clothing too many. But that's easy enough to remedy," he assured her. "Hang on a minute, okay?"

"Angelo?" She got no response. Had he put down the receiver? She heard a creaking noise. Were those... bedsprings? Surely not. Even so, her grip tightened on the lapels of her pajama top and she had to pull it out from her chest a few times to cool her suddenly heated skin.

Angelo came back on the line then. "Do you want to know what I'm wearing now, Atlanta?"

His words held a dare. She nearly backed down. *Basta.* She'd had enough of meekness.

"I think I can guess," she told him. "Hmm. Let's see. A smile?"

"That's a given. What else?"

The seductive voice that replied was one she barely recognized as her own. Even while filming a love scene on the set, she'd never sounded like this, nor had she ever felt this way around a man. Confident. Powerful. Sexy and in control.

You're worthless, Jane. Worthless. You can't do anything right. Just like your mother.

Body of a centerfold and no clue how to use it. Good thing your fans can't see into our bedroom.

She banished the ugly memories and embraced the moment instead. "You do know that that sheet is optional, right?"

"Same goes."

"I have a confession to make."

"You're not wearing a sheet."

"I'm not." She fingered the fabric-covered button

between her breasts. Before she could fathom what she was doing, she'd fished it one-handed through its hole. A second one followed before she asked, "Does this constitute phone sex?"

"No. It's more like phone foreplay. For the record, I prefer to do both in person. I can be at your villa in fifteen minutes if I don't bother with stop signs and get lucky on those hairpin turns."

"A tempting offer." She meant it. Should she say yes? She wanted to. But the power she'd felt just a moment earlier proved fleeting. Her hand stilled on the third button. "You can take your time getting here, though. The ruins aren't going anywhere."

"Sure?"

She chose to be obtuse. "They haven't in half a dozen centuries or so."

"Your next movie should be a comedy," he grumbled. She heard him exhale then and thought he might have cursed. "Let's say an hour. That will give me enough time to take a long shower of the cold variety."

They were playing with fire, Angelo decided as he hung up the phone and reached for the boxer shorts he'd just tugged off and tossed over the side of the bed. Even so, being burned was low on his list of concerns. Need held the top stop. He'd never met a woman who had tied him in such knots, and in so short a time. He was desperate to have her. More damning, he was desperate just to be with her.

It was crazy, outrageous. They'd known each other mere days, had only shared a handful of kisses and some sexy banter.

He dropped back on the mattress. No, he reminded himself. They'd shared much more than that. He'd shared his life story, laid out all of the ugly details for her inspection. She'd listened. More, she'd accepted and understood. She'd encouraged him to quit avoiding his father, to look beyond career.

What was her life story? He knew some of it from their conversations and he'd guessed a little more. To his surprise, he wanted to know it all, to return the favor of being a good sounding board. Professionally and personally, she was at the same crossroads as he. Despite his relationship with his twin, Angelo had always been a bit of a loner. He preferred it that way. *I'm scared.* At the time he'd made that confession, he'd been referring to his career. Now, it was the unprecedented press of emotions he felt where Atlanta was concerned that left him shaken.

He took his time getting to her villa, arriving an hour later than he'd planned. She was sitting at the wrought-iron table in the courtyard. She had what appeared to be a script folded open in front of her. The fingers of her right hand were curled around a tiny porcelain cup. She wore sunglasses, her lips were slicked with a sheer gloss and she'd pulled her hair back into a simple ponytail. She looked every bit as lovely as she did done up to the nines for the red carpet.

His heart knocked unsteadily, and the disturbing mix of emotions he'd spent the better part of an hour relegating to the background surged to the fore again. He took the seat opposite hers and pretended not to have a care in the world.

"Tell me that's espresso you're drinking and that there's more where it came from."

"Yes to both of your questions." She smiled. "I take it you want some."

"I do."

She set the script aside and started to rise, but Angelo stopped her by reaching for her demitasse cup and finishing off its contents.

"I couldn't resist." He set the cup back on its saucer and stretched out his legs, resting his size eleven sneakers on either side of her dainty navy-and-white skimmers. Keep it light, he ordered himself. Keep it casual. "I've got an espresso machine at home. It's this big, expensive thing that was imported from Italy. But the stuff I make doesn't come out tasting anything like yours. Maybe you should move in with me and every cup would be perfect."

Her expression dimmed. "I thought we agreed to be real with one another? That sure sounded like an old Angelo come-on line to me."

"It was. Habit." One that ensured a certain measure of emotional distance. He blew out a breath. "I'm sorry."

"Okay." She accepted his apology with a nod. "And for the record, I moved in with a man once before for all the wrong reasons. I don't plan to make that mistake again."

His gut clenched at the thought of her setting up housekeeping with someone else. Jealousy? He didn't want to think so. Curiosity was more like it. And so he asked, "Why did you move in with Zeke?"

"In part, because I thought he needed me. He did, too. Not as a life partner, not as a partner of any sort."

"But as someone to control," he finished for her.

"Yes." Her smile was sad. "That lump of clay you once referenced."

"You didn't appreciate my saying so, as I recall."

Was that really mere days ago?

"No. Despite everything, I guess I wasn't ready to

hear it, especially from someone else. The fact I allowed him to mold me is as much my fault as his."

"I disagree, but you know that. Did...did you love him?"

"Maybe. I wanted to." She swallowed and her gaze left Angelo's to focus instead on something behind him. "Even more, I wanted to *be* loved. That probably sounds so pathetic."

Not so pathetic, Angelo thought as realization dawned.

"I wanted to be loved, too," he began. "You and I just went about it differently."

Her gaze snapped back to his. "What do you mean?"

"When I'm standing at home plate, I never feel alone or...or rejected."

She covered one of his hands with her own. He could stop, he knew. She would understand how hard the words were for him to say. But he needed to say them. Aloud. Not for Atlanta, but for himself. It was time to finally accept that the great and glorious ride he'd been on for the past two decades was ending.

"When I've got that bat in my hand and the fans are chanting 'Angel, Angel, Angel,' it's not just a rush of adrenaline I feel. It's...it's validation," he admitted.

Though she said nothing, the pressure on his hand increased.

"I'm someone then, Atlanta. I don't want to lose that, but it's slipping away. It's not about being important or famous. It's...it's just about mattering."

When he glanced up she was nodding, blue eyes awash in unshed tears. "I know what it's like not to recognize your own worth and to see yourself as defined by things outside your control. But the fact is, Angelo, you do matter. You've always mattered, with or without a bat in your hand. And that will continue to be the case."

He squeezed her hand back. "I want to believe that."

"You will. It takes time. I'm still getting there."

The moment stretched as they sat holding hands. The emotional distance he'd always maintained narrowed precariously. He cleared his throat. "So, what about that espresso?"

"Sure." She rose and reached for her cup. "I'll just be a moment."

CHAPTER NINE

WHEN she was gone, Angelo scrubbed a hand over his face. Afterward, his gaze landed on the script she'd left on the table. The fact that it was upside down didn't help given his dyslexia. It took him a full five minutes to figure out the first few words.

"The Blue Flag."

He glanced up just as she placed the cups on the table. He hadn't heard her return, probably because he was concentrating so hard trying to make out the letters.

Easing back in his chair, he apologized. "Sorry. I'm being nosy."

"That's all right. It's nothing personal. Just a script I'm considering."

Glad to have something else to discuss, he asked, "Is it one of those indie projects you mentioned the other night?"

Atlanta nodded. "The title refers to a kind of wild iris that grows in swampy conditions."

"So, are you going to take it?" he asked.

"No. I want my return to the big screen to be memorable for the right reasons, and I think critics and moviegoers ultimately would have the same concerns with the story and its characters that I do."

She picked up the script and flipped absently through

the pages. "It's not a bad story. The leading role, which is what I would play, has some depth. The character is a young woman who's just discovered that she's pregnant and is struggling to come to terms with her younger sister's recent schizophrenia diagnosis. She's worried that her unborn child could be at risk for mental illness. She's also afraid to tell her husband about the baby since he basically thinks her sister, and all people similarly afflicted, should be locked away."

"How does it turn out?"

"Let's just say the ending is satisfying in a theatrical sense, but not terribly happy."

"It sounds dark." Far darker than anything Angelo could recall Atlanta ever doing. Of course, that was exactly why she was considering the script. She wanted to break free from the mold.

"It needs to be given the subject matter, but some of the scenes border on superficial and do very little to heighten the overall tension. To make matters worse, the husband's character is way underdeveloped. I can't figure out what motivates the guy, why he's such an insensitive jerk. For that matter, I can't understand why my character would stay with him."

"Maybe she's not as tough as you are. It takes guts to walk away."

Atlanta glanced up sharply, but when she spoke, it was to change the subject. "You know, we really should be going. It's sunny now, but the forecast is for rain later in the day. We should have no problem getting in our sightseeing before the weather turns if we leave now."

The ruins were indeed off the beaten path. During the last half-hour of the drive, they didn't pass so much as a roadside stand. Luckily, Atlanta had taken Franca's advice and packed a simple lunch for the two of them to share.

"Are you sure this is it?" Angelo asked after he pulled the car to the side of the road. A path opened up through the dense woods, but the only marker was a crude wooden arrow whose painted words were too weathered to read.

"According to Franca's directions. She said it wasn't a regular tourist destination."

"We don't have to go." His gaze flicked to her feet. Her shoes were practical for hoofing around the city, but not exactly designed for hiking.

Atlanta pushed open her car door. "No. We came all this way. Besides, it might be nice to see ruins on a grander scale than those in my life."

"Or mine," Angelo muttered as he joined her.

It was cooler there, perhaps because the trees blocked out most of the sun. Despite the occasional wayward branch, the path was wide enough for them to walk side-by-side. They started out at a brisk pace and maintained it even when the incline grew steeper and the ground more treacherous. Twenty minutes into the walk, Atlanta's heart was hammering, her leg muscles starting to burn and a blister had begun to form on her left heel.

"This is a regular workout," Angelo remarked, as if he could read her mind.

"Darnell would be pleased," she said, thinking of her trainer for the first time in days.

A moment later, she nearly tripped over an exposed tree root.

Angelo offered a hand to steady her. "Watch out," he warned with a laugh. "Given the shape of my shoulder,

I won't be able to carry you out of here if you sprain an ankle."

Though the words were spoken in jest, they represented a shift for him. He was no longer denying his injury and the effect it was having on him now or in the future, she thought, recalling his earlier candor about why he didn't want his career to end and his recognition that it was.

The trail ended a few minutes later at a clearing where the grass grew knee-high and was interspersed with prickly shrubs and the occasional tree. But it was the huge, grayish-white stones that commanded attention. They rose up from the vegetation like an army of ghosts, a haunting reminder of a time long past.

"It's not what I was expecting," Angelo said.

Once a fortress, it was now a pile of rubble. Atlanta had to use her imagination to picture it as it once had been, with high walls and towers and a thriving community living inside. "Nor I, but it is pretty amazing."

She rested her hands against one of the rough-hewn slabs. It was cool to the touch and partly covered in moss. Long ago, someone had labored to bring it and the others to this remote hilltop and create a wall that was intended to keep out invaders.

It had seen hard times, withstood the attacks of invaders for a couple centuries before falling into enemy hands. That was when the real damage to the structure had occurred, according to Franca. Yet part of it remained today, and it would be there long after Angelo and Atlanta were gone.

Some things defied the passage of time. The thought had her recalling what she'd told Angelo earlier about his worth regardless of his baseball career. She'd told

him he would always matter. It had been on the tip of
her tongue to add, *to me.*

It was a fact Atlanta could no longer deny.

They spent an hour strolling amid the ruins. The
view alone was worth the hike. Even with a few clouds
starting to darken the sky, or perhaps because of them,
the vista was dramatic. Atlanta leaned her elbows on
what remained of the fortress's exterior wall and gazed
down at the valley below.

"Do you really see me as tough?" she asked, hark-
ing back to their earlier conversation on her patio. She
turned to face Angelo. "And not, well, the man-eating
shrew the tabloids are portraying?"

He settled one hip on the edge of a stone and studied
her.

"You're a force to be reckoned with, Atlanta, and for
all of the right reasons."

"When I was a little girl...I...I wasn't so tough. I
vowed to myself I would never make that mistake again,
yet I did with Zeke. The circumstances were different,
but..." She shrugged.

"No one's tough when they're a kid, even if they want
everybody to believe otherwise."

"Does that include you?"

He studied the calluses on his hands, no doubt the
result of gripping a bat. "A week ago, I would have
denied it, but yeah. That includes me."

"What's different now than a week ago?"

His expression turned oddly guarded and it sounded
as if he said, "I'll let you know when I figure it out."

There wasn't much left to explore, but they stayed a
little longer. The approaching storm made the view all
the more compelling.

"I can't believe I forgot to bring my camera today," she said as, far in the distance, lightning streaked the sky.

"I've got my cell phone. It's got a camera." He unclipped it from his belt.

"Do you get a signal out here?"

"I haven't checked. To tell you the truth, I hope to God not. The only people likely to call right now are my agent, the team doctor or some reporter. I don't want to talk to any of them on this trip."

"Then why bring a cell?"

"Habit. A bad one." But then he was holding up the phone and instructing her to smile.

He glanced at the display afterward. "Gorgeous."

She dismissed his compliment with a shrug. "I'm photogenic is all."

"Actually, I don't think you look as good on film as you do in person."

She opened her mouth to dismiss his compliment once again. Instead, she heard herself ask, "Really?"

"Really." Angelo leaned one elbow against a boulder, the picture of masculine perfection. "They say the camera adds ten pounds. From where I'm standing, it's more like fifteen."

Atlanta was laughing too hard to be insulted. She attempted to slap him on the upper arm, but Angelo caught her hand before it made contact. He used it to pull her to him. Once she was in his arms, he slid his hands from her waist up to the sides of her breasts, eliciting a shiver.

"Maybe it is only ten." He leaned closer, kissed her neck. "You know I'm only kidding, right?"

"Yes, but only because the cannoli haven't caught up with me yet."

She turned her head to grant him greater access. He nipped her earlobe.

"God, I can't wait till they do. Don't get me wrong. You've got a killer body right now."

Eyes at half-mast, she muttered, "Zeke would say I'm too thin. Of course, if I gained back the weight I've lost, he'd get on me for letting myself go."

Angelo's breath was hot on her neck. "We've already established that Zeke is an idiot." His mouth detoured south to her collarbone. "You should eat two cannoli a day for the duration of your stay in Italy."

"Is that an order?"

"I know how you feel about those, so, no. Consider it more of a plea."

"A plea?"

"I'm not above begging when it comes to certain things."

At that moment, neither was she.

It was late afternoon when they returned to Monta Correnti. By that time the wind had picked up and the mass of billowing purple clouds was no longer far away, but directly overhead. Thankfully, Mother Nature waited to unleash her fury until they were almost to Atlanta's villa with the worst of the hairpin turns behind them.

Then the rain came down in a torrent. Even on high the car's wipers couldn't clear the windshield of water fast enough to provide decent visibility. Angelo navigated the last quarter-mile at a snail's pace. His knuckles glowed white on the steering wheel. When he finally pulled the car to a stop and shifted it into park, he let out a gusty sigh.

"That was an adventure, one I'd prefer not to repeat in this lifetime."

He had parked as close to the villa's main entrance as he could. Even so, with the way the rain was coming down, Atlanta knew she would be drenched to the skin before making it inside.

"Give it a minute," he said, stilling her hand when she went to unbuckle her seat belt. "It's bound to let up."

Slap! Slap! Slap! went the wipers in the quiet that followed, making a mockery of his prediction.

Atlanta glanced around the car. "I don't suppose you have an umbrella handy?"

He switched on the dome light, illuminating the rental's interior, and checked. "Apparently not. Sorry."

Slap! Slap! Slap! went the wipers.

Atlanta was a great believer in setting the scene. In her business it was vital, not only to involve those who plunked down cash to see the final product at their local theater, but to the actors as they worked to stay in character during filming. The storm, the close confines of the sports coupe and the intimate glow from the dome light—they turned the setting into something romantic rather than ridiculous.

Or maybe it was the man who was responsible for that. She'd fought this attraction since the beginning, terrified of it at first. But it was like fighting gravity— exhausting and, in the end, pointless. She glanced over to find him watching her. His hungry gaze caused a shiver and brought forth an appalling amount of need. Even as a flash of lightning rent the dark sky, followed by ominous thunder, his gaze didn't leave hers and his expression didn't change. All the while, the wipers continued to slap across the windshield with ineffective results.

"It's not letting up," she said quietly.

"No. I keep thinking it will, but…" He sounded bemused.

She moistened her lips. "You probably shouldn't drive back in this. The roads around here are difficult enough to navigate when they're dry."

"I could manage."

"I'd worry. Come in."

He sucked in a breath, exhaling as his thumbs tapped against the steering wheel. "Are you sure you want me to come in?"

They were talking about more than her providing him with shelter from the storm.

"Yes. No."

"Which is it?"

"I don't want you to leave."

He switched off the ignition and pocketed the keys. The car's interior went dark. The wipers went still. *Thump, thump, thump* went Atlanta's heart.

They stumbled through the villa's door together, breathless from their frantic dash. As she'd anticipated, they were both soaked. Angelo's shirt was plastered to his skin, outlining the hard contours of his athletic physique. Distracted, it took her a moment to realize that her own drenched clothing was providing a similar view. She tucked her arms over her chest. When she glanced up, he was watching her. He swiped his forearm over his face in a futile attempt to dry it. More rain dripped down from his hair.

"I'll…I'll go get us some towels," she said.

"In a minute. There's something I need to do first."

Angelo moved closer until barely a whisper of space separated their bodies. Slowly, he pushed the damp hair back from her face. His palms were warm against her cheeks. She savored his touch, reveled in the desire it had awakened from such a long slumber.

"You are the most beautiful woman I've ever seen." He whispered the words, almost as if he were speaking to himself rather than offering a compliment.

Atlanta swallowed.

You're a right pretty girl, Jane. The boys will be after you before long.

She refused to think about what Duke had said after that or what he'd done. She refused to think about Zeke and the face he'd turned into both of their fortunes.

Standing in the villa's dimly lit entryway with Angelo, she simply allowed herself to feel. For the first time in her life, what she felt was beautiful and feminine. It struck her as ironic, given her disheveled state. Her hair was plastered to her head. God only knew what had become of the mascara she'd brushed on her eyelashes that morning. Yet he found her beautiful and she felt the same.

Power surged through her, the origin of which she wasn't quite able to name. She reveled in it all the same. No longer was she Duke's terrified stepdaughter or Zeke's dutiful protégé. It was as if the rain had washed away the last clinging bits of dirt from her past.

She slipped out of her flats and kicked them aside. "I'm more than a pretty package, you know."

He nodded slowly, almost as if he liked hearing the clarification, almost as if he understood her reasons for offering it.

"I figured that out within five minutes of meeting you. And I'm talking about at that nightclub three years ago." He traced her lower lip with the pad of his thumb and the same lightning that intermittently streaked the sky outside shot through her.

"It took me a little longer." A lifetime, she thought ruefully.

"Better late than never."

His hands came up to frame her face and then his mouth found hers. Desperate to hold on as the kiss deepened, she fisted her hands in the wet fabric of his shirt and gave herself over to desire.

The worst of the storm had passed outside as well as in. Angelo and Atlanta lay exhausted on the metal-framed bed in her room. Like the thunder rumbling far off in the distance, her body still felt the aftershocks of their lovemaking. She'd played countless such scenes on screen and alone with Zeke. But she'd never experienced firsthand what she'd portrayed all these years.

Until now.

It wasn't just the sex, though it had been every bit as incredible as she'd hoped it would be. It was the man. His strength and his vulnerability. His generosity, not only as a lover, but as a friend. The emotions she was experiencing at the moment were every bit as new and unnerving as those earlier physical sensations. They'd been mounting since their first meeting, growing deeper, stronger and impossible to ignore.

I love you.

The words were on the tip of her tongue, begging to be said. She wasn't sure he would want to hear them, though, so she kept them to herself as she lay next to him in the dark.

She thought Angelo had dozed off until she heard him say, "You're quiet."

"Speechless is the better word."

He rose on his elbow and studied her in the dim light. "Was it...okay for you? You seemed...hesitant."

She stilled. "I did?"

"Just a little. And only at first."

The old Atlanta, weighted down with sexual hang-ups, would have excused herself and hidden away in the bathroom, mortified. The new Atlanta rolled on top of him, determined that whatever memories he took away from their time in Italy would be positive. Those were the only kind she wanted to have as well.

"Let's see what you think this time."

CHAPTER TEN

THE sun was up when Angelo woke. He stretched and reached for the woman who was responsible for the smile curving his lips. His hands found only cool sheets. He opened his eyes. The room was empty. A breeze wafted through the open windows bringing in the clean, earthy scents of the countryside. He preferred the lingering scent of the woman who was absent. He dressed and went downstairs to find her.

Atlanta was seated at the table outside, having espresso and reading another script. The cobblestones were strewn with leaves and debris, signs of the previous night's storm. She looked...peaceful. She smiled when she saw him, her expression at once that of the seductress and the ingénue.

"I was wondering when you were going to wake up. Sleep well last night?"

"I did." Partly because she'd been there beside him. He walked to where she sat and dropped a kiss on her mouth. "I liked being awake even better."

She flushed. "Me, too."

He took the chair opposite hers and nodded to the papers in her hand. "Another script?"

"Yes."

As he had before, he helped himself to her espresso. "Does it hold any more promise than the last one?"

"My character is a serial killer." She grinned wickedly. "She doesn't see herself that way, of course. She's a nurse and her victims are people who have little or no family. She thinks she's doing them a favor, relieving them of their loneliness."

There was an eagerness in her tone that he hadn't heard before. "You sound excited."

She smiled. "I guess I am a little. It's got some serious meat for me to chew. I'm only a few chapters into it, and I can already tell the characters are well developed."

"Sounds promising."

A shadow fell across her face. "The only problem is the guys who sent it to me have had a few big duds. As a result, they've had a problem attracting financing for their last few projects. If they land me, they can land a backer. I'm sure my bankability is a big part of my draw."

"What? You don't think you can handle the part?"

"I know I can." He found her confidence as sexy as her wind-tumbled hair. "Which is why I've spent the past half-hour seriously thinking about financing the picture myself."

"As in forming your own production company?"

"Exactly." Her brows rose and on a grin, she asked, "Well? Think I'm crazy?"

"I told you once you're a force to be reckoned with, Atlanta. All I can say is, watch out, Hollywood."

Her smile wobbled a little. "Thanks."

"For what?"

"For believing in me."

He nodded. "Same goes."

* * *

He left not long after that, eschewing her offer to make breakfast. Sharing a meal with her after a long night of lovemaking was just too domestic, especially since they'd spent the better part of the past twenty-four hours together. Still, it wasn't because he didn't like the idea that he declined. It was because he did…way too much.

On the way back to his villa, he stopped in town at the little coffee shop where he and Atlanta had shared cannoli their first full day in Monta Correnti. It seemed a lifetime ago. He'd changed so much since then. They both had changed, and so had their relationship. And not only because it had turned physical.

Last night, after they'd made love a second time, she'd asked him what would happen when they returned home.

"We resume our lives," he said evasively, rather than giving her the answer that had come so readily to mind. He wanted to keep seeing her, logistics and complications be damned. Things didn't have to end…in Italy.

He was returning to his car, lost in thought and balancing a cup of coffee and a pastry, when he heard his name called. He didn't recognize the raspy male voice, but he knew the speaker's identity in an instant. He stopped abruptly and he swore his heart did the same. As he turned, time reeled backward.

"Papa."

He whispered the name, but it scraped his throat as viciously as a blood-curdling scream would have. For one crazy moment Angelo was a confused and heartbroken little boy again, wondering what he and his brother had done to deserve being sent away.

I'll be good.

Bile rose in his throat. How many times had he made that promise in the days leading up to his ouster?

Now in his late sixties, Luca's light brown hair was streaked with gray at the temples and his expressive face was creased with lines. Those seemed to be his only bow to age. He remained a tall man, only about an inch shy of Angelo's six feet three, and, even though he wasn't as broad or as thickly built as his twin sons, he commanded attention. But that wasn't why he commanded Angelo's.

Papa.

He didn't say it aloud this time. He kept the name to himself. He wasn't quite as successful, however, at stopping the memories. They flashed in his head like an old film reel, a bit grainy from age, but clear enough to pry open what he'd thought were ironclad defenses. He recalled riding on his father's shoulders and climbing up on his knee. He remembered giggling riotously as Luca tossed him high in the air, and then begging for another turn after Alex had received the same treatment.

Ti amo, Papa.

Love in its purest form—that of a child for a parent—welled up. Anger, confusion, grief and fear helped banish it. They rose with the force of a tsunami to wash away the memories and the words he hadn't recalled in more than three decades.

So it was that as Luca drew even with him and broke into a smile, Angelo was clenching his teeth.

"Angelo! My son. I can barely believe my eyes." Luca smiled and extended, not his hand, but his arms, clearly expecting to wrap his long-lost son in a welcoming embrace.

Angelo took a step backward, not in retreat but to make a stand. He'd been sent away, exiled. He wasn't sure he could be as forgiving of that fact as his brother Alex was. Luca's expression faltered but he nodded as if he understood this reunion would not be so tidy after all.

"I've wanted to come by your villa after sending the welcome basket, but Isabella said I should wait, give you more time."

God bless Isabella. Even so, Angelo said quietly, "I've had thirty-five years of time."

Luca flushed. "I…I have no excuse to offer. Only an apology, which I hope that you will accept."

Angelo ignored the words. "Actually, I'm glad you didn't come by. I've been enjoying my stay."

Despite the implied insult, Luca nodded. "That is good. The company of a beautiful woman helps."

Of course he would know about Atlanta. "It does."

"Perhaps the two of you could come by the restaurant one evening and let me buy you dinner."

"I don't want anything from you."

"I only wish to buy you a meal," Luca pointed out, his reasonable tone in stark contrast to Angelo's petulant one.

He moderated his. "I'll bring her to Rosa for the meet and greet with the relatives that Isabella has planned. I assume you'll be picking up the tab for that."

Luca's expression was sad as he held out a hand in entreaty. "How I wish I could change the past."

Angelo's eyes stung. Because he wanted so badly just then to believe his father meant it, he shook his head. "But you can't, Luca. You can't."

Back at his villa, Angelo paced in agitation. Who did the man think he was acting so hurt, looking so sad and offering apologies that were three decades too late? Well, he wanted an apology even less than he wanted his old man to buy him and Atlanta dinner at Rosa.

"I don't want you in my life," he muttered. "I don't need you."

Stone by stone, Angelo rebuilt the wall around his heart where his father was concerned. If not for Atlanta, he would be packing his bags and making arrangements to return to New York. But they had plans for later. That was the only reason he was staying in Monta Correnti. Otherwise, his mission here was complete, as far as he was concerned.

He said as much to Atlanta when she arrived for dinner that evening. He'd had the meal catered, making the arrangements through Isabella with no mention of the meeting with their father, though he figured she'd probably heard about it. Just as she'd probably heard that he'd snubbed Luca's offer of dinner at Rosa. Angelo had paid in full for the meal, offering a generous tip to the young man who delivered it.

As they sat at the patio table Atlanta said, "I'm glad you're sticking around. Not just for me, for you."

He knew what she meant. On a sigh, he admitted, "I didn't think this was going to be so difficult."

"Confronting the past never is easy."

He angled his head to one side. Questions nagged. "You've never mentioned much about your family."

"That's because I don't like to talk about them," she said quietly.

"Neither do I, but I have."

She sipped her wine. "Let me put it another way. Luca is Father of the Year material compared to my stepdad."

Angelo snorted. "Right."

"Definitely. Duke was pure evil. I found it best to

make myself scarce whenever he was home, especially if my mother wasn't around."

Dread pooled in his stomach. *No. No.*

"I know what you're thinking," she said mildly.

"You do?"

"You're trying to match what I just said to the story the public has been fed."

God help him, he wished that were what he was thinking. Still, he said, "They don't add up."

"No." She sipped more wine. "My so-called humble beginnings were a little seedier than that."

"You said stepfather. What about your dad? Where does he figure in all of this?"

"He doesn't. The truth is I don't know my biological father's identity. Even my mother isn't sure. It could be one of a half-dozen different men. She wasn't terribly discriminating, especially if the guy had a few bucks in his pocket and could help her make the rent. Before she married Duke, a slew of 'uncles' lived with us.

"I don't tell many people this, of course. In fact, only one other person knows the truth."

"Zeke," he said.

"My attorney." That came as a surprise. "He sends my mother checks to keep quiet."

"What about your stepfather?"

"He died five years ago. Until then, I was sending Duke checks, too. He demanded more than my mother."

"Why?"

She said nothing, but her silence spoke volumes. It was a good thing the man was dead. Otherwise Angelo would have had to kill him.

"They blackmailed you."

"Yes." She pasted on a smile. "See what I mean. Your family is the portrait of normal by comparison."

"I wouldn't say normal, but…" He reached across the table for her hand. "I'm sorry, Atlanta. So damned sorry."

Angelo's touch, combined with the compassion in his eyes, was almost her undoing. She called on all of her acting skills to suppress her emotions.

"There's no need to be. I came to terms with the situation a long time ago. I'll never have a relationship with my mother other than as her meal ticket. She's made it clear that's all she sees me as. I never hear from her on my birthday or at the holidays. The only time she contacts me is through my attorney because she's running low of funds.

"As for Duke, I actually celebrated when I learned that he'd died of a heart attack. That's not something I'm proud of, but it's the truth." She fingered the stem of her wine glass. "I drank champagne. Half a bottle of it."

"Piper-Heidsieck?" Angelo asked.

She glanced up and smiled. "That would be the one. Not a magnum, though."

"I'd say you were entitled, even if it had been half a magnum."

"I thought so, too. Zeke was appalled when he arrived home and found me listening to old-school country music and well on my way to being snockered." She laughed dryly now at the memory of her ex pacing their bedroom and demanding answers while she'd giggled hysterically and done her best Tanya Tucker impersonation.

"Family is one big pain in the backside," he grumbled.

"I'd have to agree. Still, I wish it could be different."

At his surprised expression, she added, "I still fantasize about my mother coming to me, begging for my forgiveness and telling me that she's proud, that she cares."

"Make no mistake, Luca doesn't care. If he cared, he would have been there all of these years. Come to that, if he cared, he would have been the one to contact me and Alex, instead of leaving that chore to Isabella."

"Maybe he was afraid, Angelo."

"Of what?"

"Of your reaction. Maybe he was afraid you would reject him, again. You know how that feels."

"Don't."

But she pressed ahead. "He made a really bad choice and he knows it." Atlanta was thinking of her own poor decisions when she added, "Things like that haunt you."

He sighed. "I'm usually a pretty easygoing guy. I've been hit by pitches that were thrown with the intention of taking me out of a game. I shake it off. I've even been known to buy the pitcher a beer after the game just to show there are no hard feelings. But this..." He shook his head. "I can't get around the fact that Luca sent us away. I can't forget. I can't forgive."

"That line in the sand you once spoke of?"

He nodded. "Yeah."

Atlanta thought about Zeke and her stepfather. Both men had left her with scars, emotional, psychological and physical. Had she forgiven them? Would she ever be able to forget?

"Maybe it's enough just to move on," she said after a moment.

The meal was finished. The moon was rising. At least one of them had come to terms with the past.

"That hot tub looks inviting," she mentioned after a moment.

"Too bad you didn't bring your swimsuit."

Atlanta stood and reached for the hem of her shirt. "And here I was thinking, how fortunate."

Angelo's phone woke him the next morning. This made twice he'd slept with Atlanta. Twice he'd awoken alone. He didn't care for it, he thought as he untangled himself from the sheets to reach for the receiver. It was his brother.

"Hey, Angelo. How's everything going?"

"It's going," he answered slowly, trying to get his bearings. According to the bedside clock it was nearly nine.

"Have you spoken with Luca?"

"Yesterday, actually. I ran into him in town."

"You *ran* into him? That doesn't sound like you had much of a conversation."

"Close enough."

"Angelo—"

"Don't," he warned.

"Are you okay?"

"Why wouldn't I be?" he scoffed.

"It was a jolt for me, too, seeing Papa again."

"Don't call him that," Angelo ground out, stumbling back till he found the edge of the mattress.

"He's our father, Angelo. Like it or not, that much can't be changed. And Luca wants to be part of our lives now, whatever part we're willing to let him be."

"You know my answer."

"Then why are you there?"

"You strong-armed me into it."

Alex was quiet a moment before saying, "It was

strange for me, too, being in Italy. I didn't think I had any real memories of the place or of Luca or that part of our childhood, for that matter, until I was in Monta Correnti. Then all of a sudden bits and pieces of the past started coming back."

Angelo swallowed as some of the memories to which his twin referred beckoned. "Do you remember going out into the countryside to pick herbs?"

"Yeah." Alex chuckled. "Luca was very particular about what he wanted. I remember that he turned it into a game of sorts. Who could find the most perfect basil leaves?"

"You always won."

"Only because you were too impatient to look."

"We took turns sitting on his shoulders," Angelo said. "I felt like a giant up there."

"Yeah." They both fell silent. Then Alex changed the subject. "According to the media, I see you're not hurting for female companionship on this trip. How in the hell did you manage to meet Atlanta Jackson?"

Angelo opted to keep it light. "You know how it is, bro. No woman can resist my charm. You'd better marry Allie quick before she comes to her senses and realizes she's engaged to the wrong twin."

"Not a chance. She and I are perfect for one another." He said it with such conviction that Angelo couldn't bring himself to come back with an off-handed remark. He walked to the window. Atlanta was outside. His heart hitched seeing her, since he'd thought she'd gone.

"I'm happy for you, Alex. I'm happy for both of you."

"Thanks. I've got to say, I'm a little worried about you. There's a lot of unflattering coverage of Atlanta in the press these days. Now they're saying some interesting things about you, too."

"You know the tabloids."

"Yeah, but it's not just the rags that are reporting these things. I saw a piece on the nightly news the other day that the two of you are holed up together at an undisclosed location in Italy. Baseball fans are wondering why you're not at the playoff games, even if you can't swing a bat. When the Rogues lost the other night, a couple of fans burned your effigy."

"What?"

"They were drunk and ticketed for disorderly conduct, but they aren't the only ones who feel like you've written off your team."

"That's not true," he yelled into the phone.

"It's not me you need to convince," Alex said quietly.

"It would kill me to suit up and sit on the bench, but I've followed the games on the Internet. I've been in contact with management and my agent. Hell, I even e-mailed that rookie outfielder with some advice and encouragement."

"The fans only see what they see. And right now what they're seeing is New York's Angel tramping about in Italy somewhere with Hollywood's Mata Hari."

Angelo let out a string of curses while his brother continued.

"One report claims you and Atlanta met a few years ago. Now the speculation is that you've been seeing one another behind her boyfriend's back and you're the main reason for their breakup."

"You know me better than that. I don't poach," he growled.

"Hey, don't shoot the messenger. I'm just saying there's a lot of speculation out there."

"Well, here's the truth. Atlanta and I did meet a few years back, but she blew me off completely." Muffled laughter rumbled through the line. Angelo ignored it. "Then we ran into each other at JFK on our way here. We barely know one another," he concluded. Even without glancing at the bed, he knew he was lying.

"A waitress from the airport's VIP lounge says she saw the two of you together. She said you looked very chummy and even shared a kiss."

"It was more like a friendly peck goodbye."

"Goodbye? You're still together," Alex pointed out.

"We wound up on the same plane, bound for the same place. Pure coincidence." Or was it fate?

"So, it's nothing?" Alex said.

Angelo watched Atlanta through the window and took his time responding. "I don't know what it is."

"That sounds serious coming from you."

"I...don't know."

"You can do better than a bimbo, Angelo."

If they'd been face to face rather than speaking on the phone, Angelo would have taken a swing at Alex. His anger came through loud and clear in his words.

"Watch what you say about her."

"It's like that, huh?"

"Like what?" he grumbled.

"Serious."

"It's not serious." Liar, his conscience argued.

"Are you sure?" Alex's voice lowered then. "I told myself that when I met Allie. Love is pretty scary and at times it's damned inconvenient, but it's worth it when the woman is right."

He sucked in a breath, feeling gut-punched. "I'm not in love."

Alex didn't argue with him. Instead, he said, "Be careful, Angelo. Be sure she's the right one."

The panic he'd felt at the mention of the L-word dissipated. "She's not who you think she is. Atlanta is very different from the women she plays onscreen, and she's definitely nothing like the woman the media are portraying her to be."

"Where there's smoke…" Alex said. Another time, Angelo would have realized he was being baited. Right now, he launched his attack.

"You're wrong. She's being set up by her ex. He's bitter and controlling. She's been his cash cow for the past decade and he's ticked that she's walked out on him."

"You sound awfully…involved in her business," Alex finished after a short pause.

Angelo huffed out a sigh. "I hate seeing anyone railroaded."

"What about the affairs?"

"Rumored affairs. And the rumors are bunk. Atlanta is no femme fatale."

"Then far be it from me to argue," Alex responded quietly. "Besides, your love life isn't the reason for my call."

"I'd rather talk about Atlanta than Luca."

Alex merely laughed. "I bet you would. Have you had a chance to meet anyone else from the family?"

"Isabella." Angelo's tone softened. "She was at the villa when I arrived. She welcomed me to Monta Correnti with a feast fit for a king."

"She's all heart, not to mention one hell of a cook," Alex agreed.

"I still can't believe we have a sister."

"And a couple of brothers, too." Alex chuckled. "Wait till you meet Valentino. He's the life of the party. He kind of reminds me of you. He's a thrill-seeking adrenaline junkie, not to mention a real player when it comes to the ladies. Not that he's doing that any more. Clara would have his hide."

Angelo mentally flicked back through conversations he'd had with his brother on this topic, conversations he'd dismissed at the time but now found himself wanting to recall. "Valentino's not really our brother, though, is he? I'm talking blood-wise. He's not a Casali."

"Don't let anyone there hear you saying that," Alex warned in a surprisingly stern voice. "Valentino may not be Luca's biological son, but that's a non-issue for all involved. He's family."

Family. Alex bandied the word about with such ease.

"So, Luca could father a kid he didn't, well, father, but conveniently forget all about us?"

"That chip you're carrying around has to be hell on your bum shoulder," Alex said dryly. "Speaking of which, what are you going to do about it?"

"The chip?"

"The shoulder."

Angelo knew. He'd always known. "Surgery."

"And then?"

"I'm thinking about coaching. Or I may try my hand at commentating."

"I'm surprised to hear you say that."

"Why? I love the game. I'll always be part of it."

"That's not what I find surprising." Alex was quiet a moment. "I'm glad you finally came to this realization."

He'd had some help, Angelo knew.

He decided to redirect the conversation. "Isabella mentioned that Cristiano is a firefighter and he'd been injured in a blaze in Rome."

"Yes. Although Isabella is playing that down some-what—it was no ordinary blaze. Cristiano saved seven lives in the recent terror attacks in Rome. He's a hero. They're all very proud of him."

Respect welled a second time. Admiration followed. He found himself curious about this man, this brother, and wanting to meet him. In fact, he found himself wanting to meet Valentino. Family. When had the concept stopped feeling so foreign?

Alex's voice came through the line. "Hey, are you still there?"

"I'm here." Angelo rubbed his temple and admitted, "It's a lot to process, you know?"

"I know. I struggled with it at first, too. Allie helped me see what a gift I was being given."

"A gift." Angelo snorted.

"Give it time," Alex urged. Before hanging up, he added, "And give Luca a chance."

His brother's plea echoed in Angelo's head long after their conversation ended. Maybe their father was due a few more minutes of his time.

CHAPTER ELEVEN

HE JOINED Atlanta out by the pool. She was seated on the edge, her bare feet and legs dangling in the sun-dappled water. He settled beside her and gave her a kiss.

"I've got to tell you, I don't like waking up alone."

"Sorry. I'm an early riser. I didn't want to wake you. You looked so peaceful."

"Wake me," he said. The kiss that accompanied his request was longer than the first one. If not for the cool water lapping at his legs, he would have forgotten what he needed to say. He pulled back and cleared his throat. "There's been a change of plans for today."

"Has something come up?"

"I…I need to go see my father."

She blinked in surprise. "What made you change your mind?"

"Alex." He sighed heavily. "My brother just called. He thinks I should give our father a little more of my time."

Atlanta rested her head on his shoulder. "He's not the only one who feels that way."

"I know."

"I don't think you'll regret it, no matter what the outcome."

"The past needs to be confronted and all that."

"So, you have been listening." After giving him a kiss, Atlanta rose to her feet. "Call me later?"

"Count on it."

Despite his resolve, Angelo wound up taking his time going to see Luca, whom he knew from a call to Isabella would be at Rosa. It was late afternoon when he finally made it to the village. His footsteps faltered outside the restaurant and he jammed his hands into the pockets of his jeans. Five minutes passed and found him still standing in the same spot.

"He who hesitates…" a feminine voice remarked dryly.

He turned to find an older woman standing in the doorway of the restaurant next door. She was a stranger, but he felt certain of her identity. The infamous Aunt Lisa. The woman who'd apparently had the means to bail out her brother, but had chosen to let him send his sons away instead.

"I'm not lost," he countered.

"And yet you are still standing there." Her lips curved. She had classical features, the kind that defied the passage of time. She had to be around Luca's age, yet she remained a strikingly beautiful woman.

"I like taking my time."

"Then, by all means, carry on."

Neither of them moved. After a moment, he said, "I believe we're related."

"I believe you are right." Her gaze held a hint of amusement. "I am Lisa Firenzi."

He nodded as he mentally added another face to the list of names in his head. "You're Luca's older sister."

Her mouth tightened fractionally. Vanity, he decided. Few women appreciated having their age referenced in any way. Given this woman's sleek dark hair and fashionable appearance, it was clear she was determined to wage a take-no-prisoners battle against time.

"And you are Angelo, or, as they call you back in New York, the Angel."

"That's right," he said, and crossed to where she stood.

"I visited your city once and saw a photograph of you in the newspaper. You are quite famous, I gather."

"I'm good at what I do," he replied mildly.

Lisa wasn't fooled. "You are better than good, at least according to the newspaper clipping I read. I do not claim to know anything about this sport you play—"

"Baseball."

"*Sì*. But the article made it plain that you have many loyal fans."

How loyal? The very question that had niggled so persistently for weeks suddenly seemed unimportant. They'd remember him or they wouldn't.

Lisa was saying, "Why don't you come in to Sorella? Let me treat my famous nephew to an exceptionally fine meal."

He cast a glance back at his father's restaurant.

Lisa apparently read his mind. "Rosa isn't going anywhere and neither is Luca. Besides, I believe you might know one of my guests, a lovely young American woman who is sitting all alone." Lisa clicked her tongue. "Such a pity."

He peered past his aunt into Sorella. Atlanta was seated with her back to him at a table in the middle of the restaurant. His pulse picked up speed when he spied the familiar cascade of nearly white hair.

"I'll come in," he informed his aunt. "But I'll buy my own dinner."

"You are so like your father." The corners of her mouth turned down then and she shrugged. "As you wish."

"Fancy running into you."

Startled, Atlanta turned to find Angelo standing behind her. "What are you doing here?"

"Same thing you are. Planning to have an early supper." Angelo settled into the chair opposite hers, dwarfing its sleek chrome frame.

She lowered her voice, "So, how did it go, your meeting with Luca?"

"I haven't seen him yet."

"You've had all day," she said.

"I know."

He wasn't quite ready.

The same waiter who'd taken her order for chicken piccata came by again. Angelo requested linguine in white clam sauce and a bottle of wine. Courage, she decided.

The wine arrived at their table a moment later. Followed not long after by their entrées.

"I'm curious about something," she said. "When you spoke to your brother earlier, what did he have to say about me?"

Angelo halted mid-sip. Not a good sign, she thought.

"What makes you think we talked about you?"

She eyed him in challenge. "You didn't?"

"Maybe just a little. He read about us."

"God." Her fork clattered to her plate. "Tell me you set him straight."

"Of course I did. I made sure he knew that all that stuff is garbage." He reached across the table for her hand. "He's going to like you."

Angelo toyed with the last of his linguine as he mulled

what he'd just said. He'd never brought a woman around to meet his brother, yet he couldn't deny he wanted to introduce Atlanta to Alex and not only because he wanted his twin to see her for the woman she was, rather than the film sensation or the tabloid staple she'd become.

"You're frowning," Atlanta said softly.

"This thing with Luca," he evaded. "I don't like being at odds with my brother."

It was true, just not the whole truth. She picked up on that.

"But that's not the only reason you're out of sorts. In fact, Alex isn't the only reason you came to Italy."

"I'm looking for some answers," he admitted. Part of him wanted to make those meaningful connections he'd not only been denied, but had denied himself.

Family.

Despite his close ties to Alex, Angelo truly had never understood its importance or its staying power. He was starting to. It created connections, not only between people, but between the past and the present. Isabella and his cousins placed such stock in it they were rallying together to mend an old rift. Family also held out a promise for the future. Connections, he thought again, his mind turning to Alex and Allie and little Cherry.

"What's my legacy?" he asked softly, almost to himself.

Before coming to Italy he'd thought he knew. It was baseball—his stats at bat and in the field. It was a good bet he'd be inducted into the Baseball Hall of Fame. That kind of immortality was no longer enough.

"Your legacy is what you choose it to be." Her expression held understanding.

A feeling of rightness settled, only to be tempered by

fear. What if he loved Atlanta and she left him, too? She smiled a little uncertainly as he continued to stare.

"Are you okay?"

"Fine," he lied as emotions tumbled through him.

"You're not, but I understand."

"You do?" He swallowed, not caring in the least for this vulnerability.

"Go and see Luca. It's time, Angelo."

He should have been relieved she'd misinterpreted his thoughts. He wasn't. "We're not done with our meals."

"I'll have yours boxed and pick up the check. You can finish it at my villa later."

And finish this conversation, too, he decided. "Fine. But the meal's on me."

His act of chivalry wound up being a moot point. When he went to pay, he was told there was no charge. Damn his aunt. He glanced around to set her straight. He'd pay his own way. He wasn't sure why it was so important, just that it was.

It became doubly so when the hostess said, "It was Signor Casali. He stopped in a few minutes ago. He paid your bill."

Angelo had been irritated when he'd thought his aunt had paid for the meal. Now anger, whose origin dated back a few decades, surged to the fore. Next door, Rosa bustled with patrons. People laughed and talked over one another. Festive music played in the background. It struck him again how different the atmosphere here was compared to that next door. It was far less formal. More…homey. The thought added new heat to his anger.

He wound his way through the tables and headed to the kitchen. He stormed through the swinging doors like an outlaw looking for a gunfight. The white-coated chef whirled around and let out a stream of words in hard-edged Italian. The man clearly was not happy to have his territory invaded. Angelo was past the point of worrying about stepping on toes.

"I'm looking for Luca Casali," he announced.

The man's fierce expression subsided. "You…you are Angelo?"

"Yes."

A grin broke over the man's face. "I am Lorenzo. Lorenzo Nesta. I am head chef at Rosa. I also am engaged to your cousin Scarlett."

More ties, more connections.

"Can you tell me where to find Luca?"

"He is with Scarlett in the office." Lorenzo pointed toward a set of doors. His lips twitched a little when he added, "Maybe you could knock this time, *no*?"

Angelo had no intention of heeding Lorenzo's advice. Luca had barged back into his life without invitation. Why shouldn't he return the favor? So, when he reached the office, he turned the doorknob and sent the door flying open with enough force that it came back and banged him in his bad arm. That ticked him off even more.

"Angelo!" Luca blinked in surprise at his son's sudden appearance. The young woman sitting behind the desk appeared utterly startled.

"I came to return your money." He bit out the words.

Luca's face clouded with confusion. *"Scusi?"*

"There was no need for you to buy dinner for Atlanta and me."

"No need, *sì*. I wished to do it. I told you so the other day."

"Well, I *don't* wish you to do it. I want nothing from

you. Not a damn thing!" He pulled a wad of bills from his pocket and pressed them into his father's hand. The amount was more than enough to cover the check.

"Do you realize the insult of your actions?" This from Scarlett, who had risen to her feet and was coming around the desk. Her dark hair and chocolate eyes spoke of her Italian ancestry, but her English carried an Australian accent.

"Did he?" Angelo challenged.

"I can't believe your nerve—"

"It is all right, Scarlett." Luca held up a hand. "Angelo is entitled to his anger."

She huffed out a breath. "Is he also entitled to act boorish and ungrateful?"

"No." Angelo answered before his father could. His blinding anger had begun to dissipate. All too clearly he could see this exchange from his cousin's viewpoint. He *was* being boorish. He *did* seem ungrateful. "I apologize for barging in here. At the very least I should have knocked. The cook—"

"Chef," she inserted icily.

"Lorenzo, yes. We met in his kitchen. He's your fiancé, I believe." Scarlett's expression softened slightly. Angelo went on. "He advised me to knock first before coming in here, but I had already worked up a full head of steam."

"Over what? Your father wishing to welcome you home by paying for your meal at my mother's restaurant? Yes," she drawled. "I can see how that would offend you."

"He has more reason than that," Luca inserted quietly.

"No, Uncle, he doesn't understand—"

Luca took her hand, kissed it in a doting fashion.

"Can you leave Angelo and me alone for a moment, *per favore*?"

She looked torn, but finally nodded.

"I saw you and Atlanta through the window. I meant no offense in buying your meal," Luca began when they were alone. "It was intended as a gesture of goodwill."

Move on. Atlanta had told him that. Angelo swallowed. Some of his pride went down in the process.

"Thank you."

Luca's face brightened. "You're welcome. Did you enjoy your meal?"

"I did."

"Especially the company, I would imagine. She is a very beautiful woman."

"She's a hell of a lot more than beautiful."

"I felt that way about my Violetta," Luca mused before flushing.

"And my mother? How did you feel about her?"

Luca's expression turned thoughtful. "Your mother was lovely. She had an infectious laugh and a great love for adventure."

"She was the life of the party, all right," he replied dryly. "So, did you love her?"

"It happened so quickly."

"Did you love her?" Angelo bit out the words.

"I thought so at that time. She was an incredible woman. But life here was not what she expected. By the time she decided to go back to America, we both knew we weren't what the other needed."

"She left Alex and me here with you."

"She had a demanding career and lived in a big city. We both felt it would be for the best for you to stay here."

Twice abandoned, which made his tone all the more bitter when he said, "That was short-lived."

Luca closed his eyes on a sigh. "Of all the mistakes I've made in my life, sending your brother and you to live with Cindy is the one I regret most."

"Then why did you do it?"

"I was selling food from a roadside stall at the time," Luca began. "Money was tight. I...I had no means to keep you, no way to care for you."

He'd heard it all before from others. He still didn't understand. "So you sent us away. Even though you and Cindy had already decided we should stay here, you shipped us to Boston."

Luca nodded slowly. "I wanted you to have a stable home."

"Cindy was an alcoholic. I'm sure the stress of single parenthood didn't help. She drank her way to an early grave."

"I...I..."

Angelo didn't wait for him to finish. "A lot of nights, she didn't come home at all. Or she passed out on the floor before making it to her bed. Is *that* the stable home life you had in mind?"

Luca shook his head, looking like a doomed man. Even so, Angelo pulled forth another sharp-edged memory to hurl.

"Alex and I ate out of a Dumpster once. It was right after we ran away from the first foster home after Cindy died. We didn't like it there much."

"Alessandro mentioned that the father was not a kind man," Luca said quietly.

"Kind?" Angelo's laughter rang out bitter and harsh. "The guy would have beaten us senseless for the slightest transgression. That is, if he could have caught us. Luckily, Alex and I were fast on our feet."

Luca extended his hands palm up. "I am so sorry."

"Yeah. I'm sorry, too. Sorry that I let Alex and Atlanta talk me into coming here tonight and giving you a second chance to explain."

"Your brother found it in his heart to forgive me."

"Yeah, well, we may look alike, but Alex and I are very different people."

Luca wasn't put off. "So I can see. You play professional baseball for a living. Alessandro, he tells me you are very good at this game."

"It's more than a game. It's America's national pastime, as big as what soccer is here."

"And you are good at it." His father smiled.

Angelo let out a derisive snort. The lost young boy he'd been couldn't stop himself from bragging, "I'm better than good. I'm one of the best. I've got three World Series rings and I've been voted Most Valuable Player more than once. I'll be in the Hall of Fame someday. In the meantime, the Rogues pay me millions of dollars each season, and I make twice that amount a year endorsing everything from breakfast cereal to luxury automobiles."

"You have done well for yourself." Luca nodded. "I am pleased for you and very proud."

The words warmed him. He'd waited a lifetime to hear his father say them, which, in the end, was why he bristled. It was too late. Too damned late.

"Go to hell, Luca."

Atlanta was waiting for him just outside the courtyard the two restaurants shared. It bustled with people. Music played, laughter rang out over the din of conversation.

When he reached her, Angelo opened his mouth to speak. No words came. She stepped forward and wrapped her arms around him. It turned out no words were necessary. He buried his face in her hair and for the first time since he was a boy, he cried.

CHAPTER TWELVE

"URGENT!" read the subject line of the e-mail sent from her stylist. Atlanta opened it and immediately wished she hadn't.

"Make sure you're sitting down when you click on this link. I'm so sorry, sweetie."

Atlanta did as instructed. She sat first. Not that it mattered. Nothing could stop her from slumping to the floor once she'd read the story's headline.

"My daughter seduced my husband: Atlanta Jackson's mother's firsthand account of the star's dark side."

The accompanying photo was a grainy one of her and Duke. He had his hand on her backside and, though she recalled wanting to retch at the time, she'd smiled because her mother had told her to before taking the picture.

"Oh, God." It came out part moan and part plea. Not for the first time, her prayer went unheard.

Her first instinct was to stay curled up in a heap on the room's cotto floor. Her second one was the one she obeyed. Rising, she squared her shoulders. This time, she was going to fight.

Angelo arrived to find Atlanta's bags stacked in the entryway of her villa.

"What's going on?"

"Angelo. Thank God. I've been trying to reach you."

"My cell has been off. What's wrong?"

"I have to cut my vacation short."

"So I see." He motioned toward the bags and tried to give name to the flurry of foreign emotions hammering inside of him. The one beating most furiously was one he'd experienced before. He knew what it felt like to be left by someone he trusted.

By someone he loved.

"I've scheduled a press conference in Los Angeles for tomorrow afternoon." Her chin jutted up. "I'm not going to run away any more and let the lies go unchecked."

It made sense. He was proud of her for doing so, in fact. Though he still couldn't help feeling abandoned. So he asked, "Why now? What's being said now that you need to rush off?"

"Zeke somehow managed to contact my mother. Or maybe she sought him out." She rubbed her eyes. "I don't know. It really doesn't matter anyway. The bottom line is she's gone on the record claiming I seduced my stepfather."

"I can't believe she would accuse you of having sex with the guy."

Her throat worked convulsively. "But I did, Angelo."

"Atlanta."

He reached for her, but she shrank back. "Duke came to my bed every other night like clockwork from the day I turned eleven until I'd saved enough cash to leave for good."

It was exactly what Angelo had feared.

"Even before then, he'd started touching me inappropriately." Atlanta closed her eyes. "How could my mother not know what he was doing? She knew, damn her. Yet now she's pretending it was all my idea."

"I don't know what to say." Sorry seemed so trite in light of her revelation.

"You…you…don't need to say anything." She offered her fake Hollywood smile. He'd botched it, he knew. She needed reassurance. She needed his support. Before he could remedy his mistake, though, a car pulled up out front and a horn honked.

"Franca's husband is taking me to the airport. The sooner I confront this mess, the better. No more running. No more pretending. No more sweeping all of that ugliness under the rug. I don't give a damn about my career. If I never act again, it won't matter as long as I can look in the mirror and know I did all that I could to stand up for myself and set the record straight."

Despite her strong words, a tear leaked down her cheek.

"Atlanta." Just as she had for him the other day, he wiped it away. Before he could say anything else, she stepped away.

"I'm sorry about your family party. I wish I could be there for you tomorrow evening."

"Same goes."

"I'm going to echo what your brother said. Keep an open mind. Family, the real kind, is a rare gift. You'd be a fool to let it slip away. Your baseball career will leave you. Careers do. They're fickle, Angelo. Especially careers such as ours. Family—not my kind, but the real kind—it sticks around. So does love."

The driver honked a second time. "I've got to go."

"I'll help you carry these out." He pointed to the stack of bags.

"No. Your shoulder. Franca's husband will help me

get them." She opened the door and waved for the man to come inside. Here she was facing her problems head-on and Angelo was still trying to avoid reality.

Everything happened quickly after that. Atlanta's bags were stowed in the car's trunk. Afterward, she and Angelo stood together next to the idling vehicle.

"Have a safe trip."

"I will. Thanks."

"I'll call you."

"Please. I…I'd love to hear from you."

He brushed his lips against hers.

He stood in the driveway long after the car was gone. He didn't feel lonely, he felt empty. Atlanta wasn't merely a part of his life, he realized. She *was* his life.

"I can't make the party."

Isabella said something in Italian that sounded suspiciously like swearing, given her tone. "What do you mean?" she asked once she'd switched back to English.

"Something's come up. I'm booked on the evening flight to Los Angeles."

She cocked her head to one side and her expression turned less menacing. "Something? If you are going to Los Angeles, my guess is it's more like someone."

"Atlanta," he admitted. "She needs me."

His sister's eyes widened at that. "Is she all right?"

"No. Not yet. But she will be." His lips curved. "We're both going to be."

"I'll drive you to the airport."

Stunned, he asked, "Just like that? I'm ditching the family reunion party you planned for a woman you don't even know."

"You know her." Isabella smiled then. "And you love her."

"I...I don't..." Angelo started to deny it, but realized he would be lying. He loved Atlanta Jackson. What was more telling, though, was that he loved the woman who had once been Jane Marie Lutz. "I do."

Isabella's grin widened. "That makes her family."

Family. For so long, Angelo had found the word his foe. He embraced it now. He reveled in it.

"If I have anything to say about it, she will be," he promised.

Atlanta paced in the makeshift green room. The press was lining up in the hotel's largest conference room. Even so, some had been denied access in order to comply with the fire code. Her statement was going to be winging around the world via cyberspace and other electronic media before midnight. Everyone would know she'd been sexually abused by her stepfather and then had allowed herself to be manipulated by Zeke. The only person whose reaction she worried about was Angelo.

"We're ready for you, Miss Jackson."

She smiled at the young intern who'd come back to make the announcement.

As she had in New York, she murmured, "Show time," as she walked out the door.

Her purposeful stride and confident smile faltered when she spied Angelo standing at the bank of microphones.

"What are you doing here?" she snapped around her high-wattage smile.

"I'm being there. You know, like you've been there for me."

"Angelo, you don't need—"

He pressed a finger to her lips. "That's where you're wrong, sweetheart. I do. In fact, I can't imagine being anywhere else right now. You're too important to me."

The assembled media representatives had had enough of their whispered comments.

"Hey, Angelo. What's going on between you two?" one hollered boldly.

"This is Miss Jackson's press conference. I'm just here to lend support. Direct your questions to her, please."

They weren't put off, but they did ask the expected questions about her relationship with her stepfather. He stood beside her, proud of her courage as she offered up the ugly and unvarnished truth.

She glanced sideways at him as she finished.

"How do you feel about that, Mr. Casali?"

"I'm proud of her. She was a victim when she was a helpless kid. She's not a kid any more, nor is she a victim. As you can see, she's anything but helpless."

"Rumor has it the two of you are pretty tight these days," another reporter shouted. "What's the real story?"

"The real story? She didn't seduce me like some of the tabloid headlines claim." Some of the reporters chuckled. "But I have fallen in love with her."

Her mouth fell open and she gaped at him. "Angelo?"

"I didn't think I could fall in love. You proved me wrong, Atlanta. I love you." When she continued to stare at him, he added, "I hope to God you love me back or I'm making an incredible fool of myself."

At that she launched herself into his arms. "I love you, too."

One question made it over the din of voices. "What about your careers?"

With Atlanta in his arms, Angelo boldly asked, "What about them?"

"Some people are saying you're both washed up," the reporter went on.

"Not washed up. I'm retiring." The word was oddly much easier to say than he'd thought. "I've had an incredible career and I am very grateful to the Rogues organization, but I think it's time to move on."

"Unconfirmed reports say your shoulder—"

"I need surgery," he cut in. Atlanta had taught him how to face his worst fears. "I have a torn rotator cuff and some arthritis. I'll never be able to play at the level I used to. It's time to give some of the younger guys on the roster a chance to shine."

"What about Miss Jackson?" the same reporter asked. "Where does she fit in to your plans?"

She was watching him intently. Suddenly, he saw his future clearly.

"She doesn't fit in," Angelo said. "She's at the center of them. The heart. If she'll have me, I want to marry her. I want to make a family with her."

Family. There was that word again. This time, he understood it, embraced it.

"Miss Jackson?" The reporter was grinning now. "Can we get a comment from you regarding Mr. Casali's proposal?"

"There's only one thing to say to a proposal like that." But the reporters never heard her say the word yes. It was muffled against Angelo's lips during their kiss.

EPILOGUE

THE party with Angelo's family was rescheduled. Isabella had seen to all of the details. He expected it to be awkward. He expected to want to leave early. Neither was the case. With Atlanta by his side, he met just about every Casali and Firenzi and faced down the past that had been his nemesis for so long.

"I am glad you are here," Luca said toward the end of the evening. After his initial welcome, he'd kept to the sidelines. Now, with the party winding down, he returned to the fore.

"I'm glad I am, too."

"I know you haven't forgiven me, but—"

Angelo stopped him. "I've moved on. The past is...well, past. I'm concentrating on the future these days."

"Thank you."

"Thank Atlanta. She taught me that." But his expression softened. "You did what you thought was right at the time."

"Let's have a toast," Isabella called.

She began with Cristiano, who was being released from the hospital as well as being awarded a medal for his bravery in the line of duty.

All those assembled raised their glasses.

She smiled at Angelo when she said, "To family."

He smiled back before sipping his drink. With Atlanta at his side and the ghosts of the past laid to rest, he finally understood what the word meant.

"You are glad you came," she said a little later when she met up with him and Atlanta.

"Yes."

"And you will come back to celebrate with us again when the restaurants merge and reopen?"

His arm around Atlanta, he knew a moment of absolute peace when he said, "We'll be here."

* * * * *

Next month THE BRIDES OF BELLA ROSA
concludes.

*Tormented firefighter Cristiano Casali has shut
himself away by a secluded Italian lake—
until Mariella Holmes and her baby need his help.
Suddenly, Cristiano is forced out of the shadows and
into the arms of his future...*

Look out for
FIREFIGHTER'S DOORSTEP BABY
by Barbara McMahon

Coming Next Month

Available November 9, 2010

LARGER-PRINT BOOKS!

GET 2 FREE LARGER-PRINT NOVELS PLUS
2 FREE GIFTS!

HARLEQUIN® *Romance*®

From the Heart, For the Heart

YES! Please send me 2 FREE LARGER-PRINT Harlequin® Romance novels and my 2 FREE gifts (gifts are worth about $10). After receiving them, if I don't wish to receive any more books, I can return the shipping statement marked "cancel." If I don't cancel, I will receive 6 brand-new novels every month and be billed just $4.34 per book in the U.S. or $4.99 per book in Canada. That's a saving of 17% off the cover price! It's quite a bargain! Shipping and handling is just 50¢ per book.* I understand that accepting the 2 free books and gifts places me under no obligation to buy anything. I can always return a shipment and cancel at any time. Even if I never buy another book from Harlequin, the two free books and gifts are mine to keep forever.

186/386 HDN E7UE

Name	(PLEASE PRINT)	
Address		Apt. #
City	State/Prov.	Zip/Postal Code

Signature (if under 18, a parent or guardian must sign)

Mail to the Harlequin Reader Service:
IN U.S.A.: P.O. Box 1867, Buffalo, NY 14240-1867
IN CANADA: P.O. Box 609, Fort Erie, Ontario L2A 5X3

Not valid for current subscribers to Harlequin Romance Larger-Print books.

Are you a current subscriber to Harlequin Romance books and want to receive the larger-print edition? Call 1-800-873-8635 today!

* Terms and prices subject to change without notice. Prices do not include applicable taxes. N.Y. residents add applicable sales tax. Canadian residents will be charged applicable provincial taxes and GST. Offer not valid in Quebec. This offer is limited to one order per household. All orders subject to approval. Credit or debit balances in a customer's account(s) may be offset by any other outstanding balance owed by or to the customer. Please allow 4 to 6 weeks for delivery. Offer available while quantities last.

Your Privacy: Harlequin Books is committed to protecting your privacy. Our Privacy Policy is available online at www.ReaderService.com or upon request from the Reader Service. From time to time we make our lists of customers available to reputable third parties who may have a product or service of interest to you. If you would prefer we not share your name and address, please check here. ☐

Help us get it right—We strive for accurate, respectful and relevant communications. To clarify or modify your communication preferences, visit us at www.ReaderService.com/consumerchoice.

HRLP10R2

*See below for a sneak peek from
our inspirational line, Love Inspired® Suspense*

*Enjoy this heart-stopping excerpt from
RUNNING BLIND
by top author Shirlee McCoy,
available November 2010!*

**The mission trip to Mexico was supposed to be an
adventure. But the thrill turns sour when Jenna Dougherty
and her roommate Magdalena are kidnapped.**

"It's okay. I'm here to help." The voice was as deep as the
darkness, but Jenna Dougherty didn't believe the lie. She
could do nothing but lie still as hands slid down her arms,
felt the rope around her wrists.

"I'm going to use a knife to cut you free, Jenna. Hold
still."

The cold blade of a knife pressed close to her head before
her gag fell away.

"I—" she started, but her mouth was dry, and she could
do nothing but suck in air.

"Shhh. Whatever needs to be said can be said when
we're out of here." Nick spoke quietly, his hand gentle on
her cheek. There and gone as he sliced through the ropes on
her wrists and ankles.

He pulled her upright. "Come on. We may be on
borrowed time."

"I can't leave my friend," Jenna rasped out.

"There's no one here. Just us."

"She has to be here." Jenna took a step away.

"There's no one here. Let's go before that changes."

"It's dark. Maybe if we find a light…"

"What did you say?"

SHLISEXP1110

"We need to turn on the light. I can't leave until I know that—"

"What can you see, Jenna?"

"Nothing."

"No shadows? No light?"

"No."

"It's broad daylight. There's light spilling in from the window I climbed in through. You can't see it?"

She went cold at his words.

"I can't see anything."

"You've got a nasty bruise on your forehead. Maybe that has something to do with it." His fingers traced the tender flesh on her forehead.

"It doesn't matter *how* it happened. I'm blind!"

Can Nick help Jenna find her friend or will chasing this trail have Jenna running blindly again into danger?

Find out in RUNNING BLIND, available in November 2010 only from Love Inspired Suspense.